Also by Osvaldo Soriano

A Funny Dirty Little War
Winter Quarters

Shadows

SHADOWS

by OSVALDO SORIANO

Translated from the Spanish by Alfred Mac Adam

Alfred A. Knopf
New York
1993

This Is a Borzoi Book
Published by Alfred A. Knopf, Inc.

Copyright © 1993 by Alfred A. Knopf, Inc.
All rights reserved under International and
Pan-American Copyright Conventions. Published
in the United States by Alfred A. Knopf, Inc.,
New York, and simultaneously in Canada
by Random House of Canada Limited, Toronto.
Distributed by Random House, Inc., New York.

Originally published in Argentina as *Una sombra ya
pronto serás* by Editorial Sudamericana, Buenos Aires, in 1990.
Copyright © 1990 by Editorial Sudamericana, S.A.
Copyright © 1990 by Osvaldo Soriano

Library of Congress Cataloging-in-Publication Data
Soriano, Osvaldo.
[Una sombra ya pronto serás. English]
Shadows / Osvaldo Soriano.—1st American ed.
p. cm.
ISBN 0-679-41399-5
I. Title.
PQ7798.29.O58S5813 1993
863—dc20 92-54785 CIP

Manufactured in the United States of America
First American Edition

For a long time, everything's been coming out twisted for me: I think that now the only kind of stories which exist in the world are those that are unresolved and get lost on the road.

—Italo Calvino, *If on a winter night a traveler*

Little road, once you were lined with clover and flowering rushes, a shadow soon you'll be, a shadow just like me.

—Peñaloza and Filiberto, "Little Road"

Shadows

1 Never in my life had I been on the road without a penny to my name. I couldn't buy anything and had nothing left to sell. When I was on the train, I enjoyed watching the sun as it set on the plain; now all I felt was indifference. And it was so hot I could barely wait for night to fall so I could get some sleep under a bridge. Before it got too dark, I took out the map because I had no idea where I was. I'd traveled an absurd route, turning one way then another, then doubling back, with the result that I was either exactly where I'd begun or in some other place identical to it. The truck driver who'd dropped me off at a traffic circle told me I'd find a Shell station about two or three miles ahead, but all I saw was a stream flowing under a bridge and a dirt road that disappeared in the distance. Two farmhands riding horses followed by a filthy dog were driving some cattle—the only movement on the entire landscape.

The stream was dry. If I started a small fire, it would scare away all the insects and snakes. At least that's what I was told by the engineer who walked awhile with me after the train abandoned us in the middle of nowhere. The other passengers stayed put, waiting for someone to come and get them, but after the second night, when the ticket-collector and the engineer packed up all the food and started walking along the tracks, I ran to catch up with them. That's how I began walking.

Even if I didn't know where I was going, I still wanted to understand which way I was going. I lit the fire and went back to the road to smoke my first cigarette of the day. Night had already fallen and I listened to the crickets and stared at the stars for a while. Suddenly I thought about the time that German astronomer came to see me, indignant over Stephen Hawkins's latest theories, and suggesting I develop a program for him to calculate the gravitational trajectory of falling stars. He wanted to present it at a congress in Frankfurt, but by the time he brought me the first equations, I'd already been thrown out of the institute.

I'd been sitting at the edge of the road for a while when a pickup truck came by honking its horn, almost passing by the traffic circle. It was the last vehicle I saw, and because my hands were shaking from hunger, I went at ten o'clock to get the apples the truck driver had given me. In my bag, I had some crackers I'd taken from the dining car, but I told myself it would be better to leave them for tomorrow morning. I wanted to start out early, get something to eat, and find someone who could get me to a train station where I could get my money back for the unused part of my ticket. I could use the cash to buy some clothes—I was already starting to look like a tramp. I let the fire go out by itself, used my bag as a pillow, and smoked another cigarette before going to sleep.

I woke up at dawn and went to see if I could find someone to help me out. In the distance I saw the farmhands still stuck to their horses as if they were fused together. I needed a hot meal, a cup of coffee, or something similar to whatever it is people drink when they wake up. Seeing me come through the wire fence, one of the hands trotted over, his whip draped over his shoulder. Still far off, he said an indifferent hello and asked what I was doing around there. He listened to me looking the other way, as if whatever I had to say didn't really interest him.

"Are you the one who lit the fire?" he asked, pointing to the bridge with his whip handle.

I said I was, that I'd slept there. When he interrupted my explanation, I realized I must have really hit the skids for a farmhand to raise his voice to me like that.

"It's against the law to do that around here," he reprimanded me, as if he were the owner of the place.

We stared at each other for a while, until the other man on horseback, who must have been the foreman, came over to see what was going on.

"I only came through to ask for a drink of water," I said, and that upset both men. The second took it as an opportunity to play the part of the good gaucho and handed me a bottle of gin he was carrying in his saddlebag.

"If you like, you can brew a couple of matés before you go," he said, pointing to a kettle boiling over a fire.

I was going to refuse out of pure pride, but my guts were so dry they were starting to give me cramps. I took a drink, thanked him, and returned the bottle. The other man was annoyed about the fire or about my looks and went off shouting at the dog.

As soon as they'd left me alone, I brewed two matés, very strong and very bitter. The package was half full, so I took a handful of maté for later on. Soon I felt better. I filled a bottle with water, put it in my bag, and waved at the farmhands from a distance. My stomach was working again, which made me think perhaps that day things would start looking up.

I went out to the road and walked along slowly for a while trying to figure out where I was. Then I spotted a twisted-up sign that said SHELL 2 MILES. I told myself I might find someone there who'd take me to the next traffic circle.

2 Seen from a distance, the service station looked as if it had been prosperous once upon a time, but now it only had two pumps, one with gas oil for tractors and the other high-octane in case someone in dire need passed by. The oil they were advertising hadn't been made for years. The tire shop and the diner were closed and starting to collapse. The attendant was sleeping with his curtains closed and only the sound of a motor would wake him up.

Out in back I found a pump that spewed out a thin stream of water into a trough. I stripped and tried to wash myself with some windshield cleanser I found next to the gas pump. It made my skin burn, but if I rinsed myself off fast, I'd be able to take my first complete bath since being on the road. I gave myself a good soak sitting in the trough, trying not to make any noise, until I saw a cat looking at me from the garage door. It was black, as skinny as a cartoon cat, and showed me a mouse it was tossing in the air. I pretended to pay no attention and shaved myself very carefully, using the foam still in the tub. Without a mirror it wasn't easy, and I cut myself right next to my beauty mark. My neck was burning and I would certainly get a nice rash, but I wanted to be clean so I wouldn't frighten people anymore.

I washed my underpants and hung them from the wire. The cat decided to eat his breakfast next to me, and since the bath had made me hungry, I took out a couple of crackers and chewed them slowly to make them last. The two of us ate for a long time, each concentrated on his own affairs. There wasn't a single insect flying around us. I supposed that sooner or later someone going south would have to pass by. When he was finished, the cat stretched out in the sun and closed his eyes. It still wasn't

8 a.m., and the sky was as clear as it is on the best summer mornings. I thought it might be Sunday, which would explain why the man in the Shell station still hadn't gotten up. The possibility that some traveler might pass was slight, but I didn't want to get bitter: I'd had a good wash and even had some maté to brew up.

I started over so many times that there were moments when I felt the temptation to give up. Why, when I'd once managed to get out of this pit, did I fall in again like a jerk? "Because it's your pit," I answered myself, "because you dug it with your own hands." A chimango hawk landed on the wire near the underpants, and the cat opened one eye. At the same time, I heard the noise of a car approaching. I jumped up to grab my shirt, and the bird flew right by my head. I barely had time to put on my shoes and snatch up my jacket when a Renault Gordini with suitcases stacked up on its roof and a bumper as high as a truck's came into the flat area near the station. The body was all patched up, but the tires were brand-new, as if the car had just been repaired that morning. It jumped up the drive entrance, made a zigzag, and triumphantly pulled up to the pumps.

"*Finito!*" shouted the man behind the wheel. "*L'avventura è finita!*"

He could barely extricate himself from the seat. He must have weighed two hundred and fifty pounds, and I figured him to have survived fifty-five years of hard living. He wore filthy glasses, his shirt was sweated through, but his black shoes were well shined.

"Fill it up, *giovanotto*," he said, and to impress me he pulled out a roll of big bills.

The Gordini had been green, but now you couldn't be too sure. It sounded as though the connecting rods were going; every once in a while some dirt got into the carburetor and the chassis shook, but the fat man seemed to have total faith in his car and paid no attention to it whatsoever.

I told him I didn't work there and that I was waiting for someone to take me south. Just then the office door opened and a blond man who clearly had no illusions about his customers appeared, sheathed in the dark purple overalls of the Shell Corporation.

"Fill it up," repeated the fat man with the money rolled up between his fingers, without answering the attendant's hello.

"And what are you going to do down south, if you don't mind my asking?" He rested one leg on the bumper and the Gordini sank toward the ground.

"I'm going to Neuquén," I told him, even though I wasn't very sure myself. "Oil!" he exclaimed, raising his hands as if he'd guessed correctly. I sat down again with my jacket in my hands. The attendant slept standing up while the numbers on the pump got larger and larger and the fat man scratched his head with the bank notes.

"And you're traveling like this, hitchhiking?" he went on with a smile. When he spoke Spanish, he lost any trace of an Italian accent. I shrugged my shoulders and told him I'd lost my job.

"You can't stay around here," the blond at the pump, who'd suddenly awakened, warned me.

Then the fat man started up indignantly, as if the remark were being made to him.

"What do you mean he can't stay here? This is a public place, isn't it?" He pointed at the Shell sign, as if he were one of the major stockholders. "*Allora*, don't you care anything about the image of the Shell Corporation?"

"Give me the exact amount because I don't have any change," said the blond, who didn't seem especially impressed by the sermon, interrupting him. Then he looked at me as if I were a criminal and pointed to something behind me.

"Is that yours?"

He'd seen my underpants. The fat man took off his glasses and instantly his face became less respectable. The attendant left the gas cap on the fender and went toward the wire. I thought the fat man would never believe my explanations and concluded I was condemned to walking the countryside for the rest of my days. The fat man pointed to the gas cap and nodded his head to me. Since I had nothing to lose, I picked up my bag, grabbed the cap, and jumped onto the worn-out seat. The fat man was a little slower in getting in, but he took off as if he were driving a car with an eight-cylinder supercharged engine. He pulled onto the highway with a rather elegant maneuver, slipped it into third, and kissed the medal he was wearing around his neck.

"*Signore, ti ringrazio,*" he muttered. On the dash, he had a decal of Carlos Gardel and a little print of the Virgin of Luján.

"He'll call the police," I said.

"There's no telephone. Never go to places that have telephones. Was that rag yours?"

"I'd just washed it."

He laughed for the first time. Then he exchanged his regular glasses for sunglasses and offered me a cigarette. I settled back in the seat, lowered the window to blow out the smoke from the first puffs, and relaxed. Outside, the air seemed like clear water.

"Were you serious about going south?"

"To Neuquén."

"Right! Oil you said."

"No, no. Software."

He tried to shift into fourth, but the motor wouldn't stand for it, so he went back into third. He moved his head from one side to the other, annoyed, while his shirt got wet over his stomach.

"*Finito,*" he repeated, his cigarette in his lips. "*L'avventura è finita.*"

"Are you Italian?"

"My last name is Coluccini. If you talk to people in a foreign language, they instantly lower their guard."

"Do these things always go your way?"

"Almost always. You've got to flash the roll, of course."

He showed me the roll: the first was a big bill, but underneath it was just slips of plain paper.

"Ingenious."

"And God helps me a bit. I came to Argentina in '57, when I was a kid, and began with a circus in Paraná. After a while, I saved enough to buy another in Bahía Blanca, and eventually I controlled the whole south. What do you think? Look at me now."

I did. He didn't look like a success.

"What happened?"

"What happened? The whole country turned into one big circus, so mine was no longer necessary. *Finito!* I'm not stopping until I get to Bolivia!"

I was silent for a while, trying to figure out if he was just kidding me.

"A circus with animals and everything?"

"What do you think? The only real lion in the whole country was mine. It was the last thing I sold in Chile."

"And now you think you're going to get to Bolivia in this?"

"What else? Once I had a Buick and a Peugeot Five-oh-five too, but the economic crisis wiped me out. Excuse me for butting into your affairs, but you lost everything too, didn't you?"

"Everything. Why don't you go back to Italy?"

"For the time being, that's out of the question. Now the idea is to get to Bolivia. After that Rio or Miami. It's in God's hands."

He kissed his medal again and sat there with his eyes glued to the center of the road.

"Going to set up another circus?"

"No, I'm too old for that. I was an acrobat and magician, but now I need glasses and have back problems."

He was starting to get under my skin, and I wasn't about to let him arouse my compassion. Besides, I remembered he was going north, and I wanted to go south.

"You can drop me at the first intersection."

"Whatever you say, but I'm going to take a side road. No sense in asking for trouble. Who knows if that guy back there managed to get in touch with the police, and you forgot your underwear."

3 For more than two hours we drove along a dirt road. When we finally hit asphalt, it looked like a line drawn to infinity. A yellow Bedford which had lost two wheels was leaning over a ditch, waiting to be rescued. Coluccini turned right and slid onto the highway. As soon as he saw us, the driver began waving his arms, and the fat man pulled over into the trailer's shadow.

"I've been here for fifteen hours," said the truck driver, who was shorter than a jockey. "Going to Colonia Vela?"

Coluccini had a habit of nodding his head from side to side, or maybe he was just shaking off his perspiration.

"Nonstop to Bolivia," he said, and instantly, as if he'd forgotten something, he added: *"L'avventura è finita."*

"La Paz or Santa Cruz?" asked the driver, who seemed knowledgeable.

"Whichever is closer. Ever been there?"

"Can't say I wouldn't want to. The problem is the family."

Right then and there, I realized I was going to be excluded from the conversation. I tried to identify a point of reference along the road, but it was all the same: wire fences, cows, the occasional tree, a dumb cloud drifting along.

"Where is Colonia Vela?" I asked the driver, who was complaining about having two kids in school or something like that. He pointed a finger into the horizon, and then told the fat man he had a friend in Bolivia who was doing very well. That revived the conversation, and I got out to stretch my legs and screw on the gas cap. The Bedford's axle had left a long scratch on the blacktop. It was one of the first models manufactured in Argentina, from '58 or '59, and wouldn't last much longer. The dual rear wheels, which had flipped off, were lying in a hay field as smooth as tiles. I walked around to see what the cargo was. I climbed up a railing and, without pulling too hard, extracted a pair of watermelons. When I got back, I saw Coluccini pounding on the steering wheel, trying to convince the truck driver to sell everything and come with him to Bolivia.

"The cargo's not mine," said the driver. "It's from San Pedro, belongs to a guy named Rodríguez."

"How much is it worth?" asked Coluccini.

"Ten million pesos easy."

"And throw in another five for the truck," added the fat man.

"At least, but we'd be locked up for sure," said the driver, laughing. "Just tell them over in Colonia Vela to send me some help."

"I can bring you there, if you like. When Rodríguez finds out, we'll already be a thousand miles away from here."

"And what about my family?"

"Bring them along later, man. Know what they need in Bolivia? Argentines, and they pay them top dollar."

Silence reigned. The fat man had taken off his sunglasses, and the driver was staring at him with his mouth hanging open, standing under the blazing sun.

"Think so? And just what line of business might you be in?"

"My friend Zárate and I," he explained, motioning toward me, "are in software."

I was just about to say something, but if I did, I'd be sentencing myself to travel by foot. Coluccini didn't get out of his car, and the other man was concentrating on his family and top dollar in Bolivia.

"I don't know, I'll have to think it over," he mumbled.

"Okay," said the disappointed fat man, without saying goodbye as he pulled away in the direction the other man had pointed toward. As he was shifting into third, he passed me a knife and asked me to cut him a slice of watermelon.

We opened the windows and drove slowly, silently spitting out seeds until I asked him who Zárate was.

"Oh, Zárate!" he answered, as if I'd touched an old wound. "A partner I used to have who's in Australia now." He pointed his thumb back and added, "That poor bastard's going to die there."

"Who'd he sell his merchandise to?"

"Another trucker. The ones who pass by empty have money and make deals with the less fortunate, who are left on the road. This country's rotten. *Finito*. Listen, for a while now I've been wanting to ask you something: what is software?"

"Programs that make computers do what you want them to do."

"And you think you're going to save yourself with that?" he asked in surprise.

"I don't think so. While I was in Europe I was doing fine, but for some reason I came back. And, just as you say, it's a little late."

"No! Never give up!" he shouted, and he seemed sincere. "Just look at me. I'm an old driver, Zárate. On the road, just when everything seems lost, there's always one last maneuver. A twist of the wheel, a downshift, something, but never the brakes. You touch the brakes and you're finished."

"My name's not Zárate."

"Excuse me. I haven't heard anything about him for such a long time . . . we were together through thick and thin. Mostly thin, bah. One day Zárate comes to me and says, 'Fuck your circus, I'm going to Australia.' And he took all of them with him: my wife, the kids, the clown. . . . They all saved themselves."

"Why didn't they take you?"

A hint of a shadow passed over his face. A grayness that came from the poplars bordering the road. He put on his glasses and remained silent until we came to the crossroads at Colonia Vela.

"Good luck," I said. "And stay out of trouble."

"Don't worry."

I put the watermelon in my bag, shook his hand, and walked toward a bus stop where a woman and two kids were waiting.

"Listen!" he shouted to me through the window. "If you get to Bolivia some day, look me up through American Express."

"It's a deal," I said, and I watched him drive off. The Gordini's noise went on buzzing in my ears for a good while.

The bus from Rauch arrived fifteen minutes later. I thought I had nothing to lose by talking to the driver, so I combed my hair as best I could. I got on after the woman and her kids, and when the man asked me where I was going, I said to the train station but that I had no money to pay him. He looked at me in the mirror and told me to sit in back, in an aisle seat.

"If the inspector gets on, I'll signal you, and you get off right away," he said. He was about twenty, with light brown hair, and wore a handkerchief around his neck. I thanked him and sat down. Almost all the passengers were farmhands from the ranches, and there was only one man wearing a suit; he greeted me, wanting to strike up a conversation.

The first large business we passed sold tractors. Later on there was a repair shop where a racing car was being tuned up, and then a supermarket with two guards and a long barricade at the door. The one-story houses with no front yard had lost the prettiness they once had. It must have been during the hours when electricity was cut off, because the only stop light on the main street wasn't working. The bus stopped twice to drop off passengers, and when it reached the plaza, the driver signaled me to get out. Before me was a closed-down movie theater, and on the corner were the Banco Provincia and an insurance company. To my right I saw a church and on the other side of the plaza a hotel and a bar open for business.

I was hungry and wanted to splash some water on my face. I took advantage of the fact that there were benches under the trees in the plaza and sat down to cut the watermelon. If I'd thought to pick up an empty tin can, I could have brewed maté. I would also have needed a spoon and some newspaper to start a fire. I poked through the trash basket, but I saw nothing I could use. Opposite San Martín's statue there was a stone tablet, and beyond that a fountain. I made sure the caretaker wasn't around

and soaked my face. I hated walking around without underpants
because it made me feel naked. My brown suit was surviving the
grime from the street, but my shoes were white with dust, and
I'd lost a shirt button.

I walked under the Liberator's saber and searched for a sharp
edge I could use to cut the watermelon. I went over to the stone
tablet, which had a nice cement point, read a name and below
it an inscription that said "Fallen in the War to Recover Our
Malvinas Islands." Since I found nothing better, I used my belt
buckle to cut it and then stretched out on the grass to eat. I
wondered if Coluccini would reach his Bolivian paradise or if
he'd end up in a jailhouse in some hick town. I wasn't certain
he was Italian or even if he'd owned some circus, but I was sorry
he wasn't going in the same direction I was. When I looked up,
I saw a priest crossing the plaza in the direction of the church.
He was hatless, but seemed indifferent to the sun. He crossed
the street and took out an enormous key ring he used to unlock
the main door. After a bit, a hearse pulled up, and behind it
four cars out of which emerged men in suits and two women
with their heads covered. The men took out the coffin and carried
it into the church. Then I heard organ music and by the time
I'd finished eating, they all left with the deceased for the cemetery. The cortege drove off, and everything became calm again,
as if there were a curfew. I nodded off for a while and then,
because there was no one on the street to see me, I cleaned off
my shoes on the grass before going into the bar to ask where the
station was.

4 The bartender, who also owned the place, was from Spain, Galicia to be precise, and spoke as if he'd just gotten off the boat. Like all men who stand on the other side of the counter, he liked to talk, and he instantly took an interest in my case. He wanted to see the train ticket and complained about how badly everything was going before informing me that the spur line to Colonia Vela had been pulled up and that the station had been closed for over a year.

On banking days, the bar must have been the place where the local ranchers and businessmen met, because there were no women or young people in sight. Somewhere behind the freezer a generator was making as much noise as a motorcycle. In the back of the bar, there were tables where customers could play cards—*mus* and *truco*, no doubt—and two billiard tables left over from better times. The Spaniard asked me if I wanted something, and I told him the truth, that I didn't have a peso to my name.

"The thing is that in this country nobody wants to work," he commented and turned around to make the two espressos the waiter had ordered.

I'd heard that before. I breathed in the smell of the coffee in the espresso maker's steam, and when the owner wasn't looking, I took a few sugar cubes from the counter.

"I didn't mean you by that," added the Spaniard, confident I was still there waiting for his mercy, "but nowadays it's fashionable to be poor. Go take a look at the chapel: people don't go there to pray anymore; they go to eat for free. Kids only know how to beg, and the government's tied the hands of the police. You have no idea what happened to the supermarket over here. They didn't even leave the toothpicks."

"Do you think I might be able to get a job?"

"Listen"—he turned around with a coffee in each hand—"the only people who aren't working are those who don't want to work."

"And where should I look?"

"I don't know, check out the area a little bit. . . . Have any family around here?"

I said I had a daughter in Spain, but it didn't move him in the slightest.

"Leaving the country is all the rage," he told me, and he served a Cinzano with a twist of lemon to a mustached man who'd come to the counter. He was one of the coffin bearers, and since the two of them had fallen deep into conversation, I realized I'd better be on my way.

"There's a truck driver stranded on the road," I said before leaving. "Can you tell someone to send help?"

"Is he from here?"

"What's the difference? He's out there baking in the sun."

"Castelnuovo takes care of trucks," said the man with the mustache, showing me a mouth full of peanuts and french fries.

Before crossing the plaza, I asked where Castelnuovo was. I walked a couple of blocks in the shade until I found the street the bus had used to enter town. After that, I walked by the Union and Progress Club, which was barely a bar with a soccer field next to it. There I was told to keep going straight until I came to a pharmacy and then turn left, following the irrigation ditch. At one corner I found a discarded beer can, but it was of no use to me because it was the flip-top kind and didn't leave enough space to stick in a spoon. I had no spoon in any case, so I kicked the can aside and went on walking until I found the dirt road.

Castelnuovo had a little repair shop and a parking lot where the trucks passing through were supposed to stop. I clapped my hands, and for an instant I imagined myself like an old-time night watchman shouting "Hail Mary!" I must have smiled, but I was actually in a bad mood. I took a look around the shop until

a pain-in-the-ass of a dog came out to scare me off and I was
forced to retreat to the sidewalk. A little while later a woman
about forty years old appeared. She'd just awakened and asked
me what I wanted. The dog stood next to her, barking and
wagging his tail. I shouted to her that out on the highway someone needed Castelnuovo's services, and she, also shouting, answered that Castelnuovo was dead and that truck drivers were
ungrateful sons of bitches. I didn't know what to say. I spread
my arms and looked from side to side to see if any neighbors
were watching us. To be done with the matter once and for all,
I told her it was a Bedford with a load of watermelons, a couple
of miles along the road, and she wanted to know where I'd left
my truck. I said I had no truck, but since I was fed up with
talking long-distance like that I said good-bye. No sooner had
I turned my back on her than I heard a shout and the sound of
running. I tried to get out of the way, but the dog managed to
sink his teeth into me, just behind my ankle, and keep on running, furious, barking at the trees while the woman shouted "Be
still, Moro," without leaving the doorway of her house. But
what bothered me most was that my trousers were torn. Now I
really did look like a tramp and would stand out wherever I
went. I felt ridiculous, and instead of bending over to see the
wound, I asked myself what I was doing standing there involved
in the lives of truck drivers, bitten by a useless dog in an unknown town while my daughter wrote me letters to a general
delivery that I might never reach. Limping past vacant lots, I
retraced my path in the shadow of the poplars that flanked the
irrigation ditch. The dog was running madly, raising dust, and
he again passed me by before going into the shop. Castelnuovo's
widow must have hit him with something hard because the animal yipped and then the silence returned. I sat down on the side
of the road and took out my handkerchief to clean the wound.
It wasn't serious: he'd caught me a glancing shot with one tooth,
and it hardly bled. A boy passing by with a soccer ball stopped
on the other side of the street to look at me. I smiled at him,
but I realized I was blushing.

"Are you tired, mister?" he asked and then bounced the ball on the ground.

I answered that I was, but since I didn't want to frighten him, I immediately stood up and told him it was nothing. The kid's ball was plastic made to look like leather. When I was a boy, I had one made of rubber that bounced better than his, although all balls are irresistible. When he bounced it off the wall, it came toward me, so I flipped it up with the tip of my shoe and headed it back to him. Then I felt pain in my ankle and hopped over to his side of the street. The boy asked me if I'd gotten hurt playing, and I just had to laugh.

We walked along together, the boy whistling and me trying to walk properly. I asked him where he lived and he said over there, near the meat-processing plant. Then he told me his name was Manuel and that he was a forward in Union and Progress's junior league. He must have been eleven or twelve, and he handled the ball quite well. As we walked, he kept it bouncing off his head and then let it roll down his back as if it were tied to his body.

"Were you always lame?" he finally asked in a respectful tone.

I told him what had happened with the dog, and he asked to see the bite.

"Holy cow, your leg's turning blue. Do you live far from here?"

"I'm just passing through."

"Come over to the club so someone can put a bandage on your leg. It's right over here."

It was almost 5 p.m., and little by little the street began to come to life. There were country people on bicycles, pickups carrying farmworkers who were getting ready for the dance, and a few cars, all driven by men. On the corner with the supermarket, a policeman stood in the shade with a cigarette dangling from his lips. From time to time, he said hello to the passersby he knew. Before we passed the guard, the boy crossed the street, pulling me by my jacket.

"This is where they arrested my father," he said, adding with a certain pride, "There's a photo of him in the supermarket window."

We went on in silence until we reached the club. It was a bare field, virtually without boundary markers, surrounded by a broken wire fence, and containing flimsy wooden dressing rooms. On the field, a few boys in sneakers were kicking the ball around, coached by a paunchy man wearing a cap with the colors of the San Lorenzo soccer team from Buenos Aires. The boy left his ball with me and ran over to the coach. It all seemed to be taking place at a distance, as if it were happening to someone else or as if I were seeing it in a movie. The trainer came to take care of me, which I let him do without going into a detailed explanation. We went to the dressing room, and he made me lie down on a table while the kids crowded around to see what was happening.

"If I were you, I'd get a vaccination," he said while he cleaned me off with alcohol. Then he put on a tight bandage and convinced me to rest until after the match.

Once they'd left me alone, I made a pillow with the towel and fell asleep instantly. I woke up two hours later, when the boys came to change. The trainer ordered them to take a shower, told them they would be eating at the chapel and to wait for him next to the pickup. When they were gone, he asked me if I felt better, and without wasting time on formalities, wanted to know how long I'd gone without eating.

"I don't know," I said. "Quite a while."

"Come on," he said, "the priest will give you a bowl of soup."

I climbed into the truck with the boys, and since they asked me so many questions about where I came from and where I was going, I told them that when I was young I'd played wing for Banfield. At first they didn't believe me, but when the boy who'd brought me to the club told them I controlled the ball really well, they asked for more details, and one of them asked me how many penalty kicks I'd blocked in my lifetime.

5   The chapel was made of bare bricks and was still unfinished. It was on the other side of the station, near a neighborhood of adobe houses. Night had yet to fall but there were already lots of people lined up at the door. The coach parked the truck in a meadow, and the boys distributed the forks and spoons they took out of a trunk.

"When you finish, just give your utensils to any one of the kids," he said.

I thanked him and got on line without even thinking about what I was doing. Some of the boys were setting up tables near a cook stove in the yard, and the priest, who was in shirtsleeves, helped carry over a basket of bread. I waited for half an hour resting on my good leg until a huge dark-haired boy who let people in a dozen at a time shouted that we could enter. I did what the others did; I grabbed some bread, served myself from a pitcher of broth, and took a plate of greens. The table where I happened to sit wobbled, and a skinny man wearing a T-shirt told me to prop it up the best I could because he couldn't spear the few carrots dancing around in his broth.

Those present spoke little, glancing furtively at each other. I ate slowly so I wouldn't burn my tongue, wondering if anyone had bothered to call in the driver. Suddenly someone shouted that his bread had been stolen, and a fight broke out, and even the priest got involved. The yard was illuminated by gas lamps that attracted bluebottle flies and lightning bugs. The man in the T-shirt told me he came from Catamarca and asked me if I too were going down to Río Turbio. I told him I was going to Neuquén and he was slightly surprised, but he quickly made an ambiguous gesture, as if to say "It's your business" and went to see if he could get seconds.

I found a piece of sausage among the greens, a discovery that made the others both amused and envious. I couldn't share it because it was only a mouthful, so I savored it along with the last potato. Then we all got up to wash our dishes and assemble for prayer in the chapel. I didn't remember any prayers, but the priest blessed us and commended us to God's care, without any sermonizing. On the way out, I returned the silverware to the boys and went to take a look at the abandoned train station.

At one time it must have been a handsome building, with cast-iron columns and stained-glass arcades. Now there was nothing left but the filthy floor where some vagrants and other people passing through were sleeping. The benches on the platform had all been torn out; not even the bell that announced arrivals and departures was left. On the wall I read graffiti that said the priest was a queer. Tall, ungainly plants that would soon cover everything were growing between the tracks. I sat down on the ground, opened my bag to see if the watermelon was still edible, and ate the last piece. I'd eaten something hot for the first time in many days and I told myself that tomorrow I'd find something else. Later I lit a cigarette, but when I realized I was the only one smoking, I put it out so no one would get jealous. The bite was making me a little uncomfortable, but the bandage was in place. I still didn't know if I could walk a long distance, though I had to get away from there. The rails were clearly visible because the moon was full, so I went down to the rear of the platform, walked down some stairs and jumped over the ties. My leg was okay, so I relit my cigarette and left Colonia Vela. The more I thought about Castelnuovo's widow and her hatred for truck drivers, the more I suspected that the man from the bar had played a trick on me by sending me to see her. His carefully clipped mustache and the way he talked with his mouth full came to mind, but I thought about other things because I didn't want to burden myself with useless anger.

There was a car with its parking lights on at the first level crossing I saw, so I hurried up to ask for a ride. As I came closer, I could hear a conversation in which a man of a certain age was refusing to say good-bye to a younger woman who had a date with another man. The car's overhead light was on, so I could make out the man's gray hair; I hid on the embankment so I wouldn't disturb them. She begged him not to come back, but he insisted on seeing her, even if it was only at Mass and from a distance. He'd be happy with a smile and a wave from afar. I heard him say that and was afraid for him. I was going to move on, but I felt the need for company, so I stayed crouching behind the weeds. Every single thing they said came from a TV soap opera, but to me their conversation sounded sincere because it was accompanied by unrepeatable gestures and pain. None of their words intended to hurt, but uttered in that manner, for the last time, at a desolate railroad siding, they would be hard to forget. After an instant of silence, I raised my eyes and saw the man's face contorted with anxiety. A lock of steel-gray hair fell over his forehead, and the shine of his eyes impressed me as much as if I'd been inside the car. It took her an eternity to say no. Then a freshly lit cigarette flew through the window. The man went on begging her, but the door opened all the way and some very high heels sank into the dust. I told myself she'd never be able to wear those shoes again: I saw her walk toward a small woods where another car, concealed by the bushes, was waiting. She was plump, but she walked with determination, putting her handkerchief back into her purse. She didn't want him to follow her, and he didn't. The second man backed his car out without using the headlights, turned toward the town, and drove away. Perhaps they did this every night or perhaps it really was the last good-bye. The first man stayed there clutching the steering wheel, immobile, as if he were hypnotized. I walked down to the road and picked up the cigarette, which was on the ground half-consumed. I looked at him again. He had a smooth, insipid face, the kind you forget instantly. He rested his head against the glass and stayed that way awhile, pensive or half asleep. Finally I heard a noise and it seemed to me he was having a drink. I picked up my bag and crossed to the other side of the road so he could see me coming. Then I realized the car was a brand-new Jaguar with a flat tire. I was suddenly curious to know if this man's bad luck might in some way change my own.

When he saw me, he started the motor and turned on the headlights, but I pointed to the tire and walked closer, trying not to limp. In my pocket, I carried the last cigarette she'd smoked while sitting next to him in the Jaguar.

6   His eyes, as he listened, were tired, his expression incredulous. Yet he seemed convinced that anything might happen to him that night. He held a glass in his hand, and the bottle was on the seat where the woman had been. The car was better tuned than Coluccini's, and I could have survived for a year on the provisions he had in the backseat. I stood about six feet from the window and offered to change his tire if he'd take me away from there. He didn't react, so I held out my identity card to him, but he made no attempt to take it. Even with a mustache, whiskers, or sunglasses, that face would still have been utterly forgettable. He took a big swallow and then dried his lips with the handkerchief peeking out of his jacket pocket.

"You're not from . . . ," he asked and looked toward some sign that might remind him of the town's name.

"No. Just passing through."

He poured himself another whiskey and unwrapped a chocolate bar with a Swiss or Italian label.

"We'll have to change the tire," I said.

"Is it really all that necessary?"

I got the feeling the things of this world really upset him.

"You must have run over a nail."

"Suppose we go somewhere and have them take care of it. . . ."

"You just can't drive on it," I insisted, "you'll ruin the casing."

That upset him even more. The motor was still running, but he paid no more attention to it than he did to the mooing of the cows. He finished the chocolate, again wiped his lips with his handkerchief, and finally remembered me.

"I wouldn't want to put you out," he said.

I waited awhile for him to get out, but he remained self-absorbed. Perhaps he was thinking about her, resigning himself to a future of seeing her only from a distance. I was starting to get nervous and told him either to open the trunk or let me do it. Only then did he turn off the motor and hand me the leather key case. Next to the spare, I found a flashlight and the jack, so I sat on the ground and got to work. I was on the third nut when he came to see what I was doing. He was carrying two glasses and a bottle of Johnnie Walker Black Label.

"A drink will do us good," he said.

He poured me a good-size shot and then leaned against the car. The jack shuddered a bit and then became steady.

"Are you a mechanic?" he asked, looking around as if he were expecting a ghost to appear.

"No," I said, "anyone can do it."

"Anyone . . . Where have I heard that before?" he said, evidently thinking about something else. He was wearing a gray suit with discreet pinstripes that must have cost a fortune. I wondered where he could have met the woman and if it had been worth his while driving all the way out here to see her. The license plate was yellow and had the letters RJ before the numbers.

"Have you had any dinner?" he asked, pouring himself another.

"A little, yes." I held the wheel in place with my legs and tightened the nuts. He watched me work with a guilty expression on his face. He waited until I finished, got back in, and invited me to join him. He straightened his tie, handed me the bottle, and made a minor adjustment to the rear-view mirror.

"Where are we?" He became interested and stared at a wrinkled sheet of paper on which a woman's hand had drawn a highway and the crossing.

"This is Colonia Vela," I informed him. "We're about twelve hundred miles from Rio de Janeiro."

He shot me an alarmed look, as if he'd surprised me going through his personal papers.

"It's that I like to drive," he said, starting the motor. "Once I was in Alaska, and then I turned up in Kuala Lumpur. I don't remember ever getting on a ship."

"How'd you get back?"

"I don't remember. I've got an empty space here." He touched his forehead. "I'm missing ten years."

We turned onto a dirt road without saying another word. I lit a cigarette, and by the light of the match I saw that next to the hand brake he had a short-barreled revolver. On the floor, there was a bit of everything: aspirin, shaving cream, several bottles of beer, cartons of Winstons, and before the light went out, I saw an open velvet-covered box and a bouquet of violets. On a card tied to the bouquet with a red ribbon, I managed to read "With all my love, Lem," or something like that.

"The highway's in the other direction," I said, just to embarrass him a bit.

"Think so?" he flinched, instantly making a U-turn. The Jaguar raised a dust cloud and skidded into a narrow rut. It bounced quite a bit, although inside you could barely tell. From what I could see of the gauge, we were going to need gas very soon.

"Going south?" I asked.

"Further south? What for?"

"I don't know, I thought you might have been going to Bariloche and got lost around here."

"Bariloche's not for me," he answered. He kept his eye on the road, but he always reacted too late to miss the potholes.

"Sorry," I said, "I didn't mean to pry."

"Don't worry. I was told there was a casino around here, and I wanted to find out about it."

"Around here?"

"I don't know, a place where they don't keep a list of the people who always win."

"Is that how you got all this?" I made a gesture that included the car and everything in it.

"No, no . . . there's no way to control roulette. You'd have to have a computer to beat it."

"Not even that would help," I said. "You'd need a year's worth of information even to try it."

He opened the glove compartment to put away the revolver and handed me a worn-out red notebook. It was filled with numbers, hours, and dates. He'd drawn a circle with green ink around 17 and 21.

"Calculating probabilities," I said. "There are dozens of books on the subject. Problems start when the casino changes the wheels. If they're changed from one table to another, it's impossible."

He stared at me with interest. He was still grieving, but now he had something else to think about.

"Imagine the wheels are all marked, and that you know which one is which as it moves from one table to another."

"If they always rotate them in sequence, then it doesn't matter which table a wheel is on."

"Wait a minute! You're an expert!" He was surprised. "How come you look like such a mess?"

I told him the story of the train and a few details about what happened later, but all he wanted to know was if I really was a software engineer.

"I don't have my diploma with me, but I know something about it. I worked for a while in France and in Italy."

"Fine. What do you say we get something to eat?"

"Where?"

"I don't know. Look on the map."

I turned on the light and searched for something that might look like a town. The car bounced along, and we got further and further from the asphalt. Then I saw a wooden sign lying on the ground that said TRIUNVIRATO 3 MILES and looked at my watch. It was almost midnight.

"I don't think we'll get anything to eat at this hour of the night, but something's going to have to be done about the tire, you wouldn't want . . ."

"Listen, I can't have that much bad luck," he said. Then he thought it over for a moment. He must have changed his mind, because he pulled over to the side of the road. "Yes, you're right. Today every number I play comes up bad."

7 Triunvirato consisted of a single street and a plaza identical to the one in Colonia Vela. A street light burned at the entrance to town and that was all. Opposite the bank, we saw a boardinghouse, and Lem stopped to get a room. I suggested we sleep in the car, but he said he was too old for that sort of thing and knocked at the door. After a while, a man came out pulling up his trousers, rather put out, to tell us that he only had one room available. I asked if there was a tire-repair shop and he pointed to a shed with a pitched roof on the other side of the plaza.

"You take it over," Lem said. "I have to make a call."

I started up the Jaguar and drove around the plaza. I stopped opposite the shop and blew the horn a few times until a boy with no shirt on interrupted a game of cards with his friends and came outside. I asked him to fix the tire and take care of the car until morning. It took him a while to recover from the shock; he told me he'd never seen a car like this and ran his hand over it as if he were caressing his girlfriend. I waited for him to open the garage door and then parked the car next to the wall where the tools were stored. I took the revolver out of the glove compartment, put it in my pocket, and turned on the overhead light to take a look at whatever else was in there. The car was registered in the state of New Jersey to a certain Lemmond Stanislas Cohen. On the backseat there was a pile of brand-new suits, cans of beer, instant coffee, several Simenon novels in French, and provisions enough for a trek across the desert. I put the notebook, a few packs of cigarettes, and a bar of chocolate in my bag. Then I took the flat out of the trunk, locked the doors, and pocketed the keys. I said hello to the boys who'd come over to admire the Jaguar, and walked back onto the street. The whole police force was sitting in an old Ford Falcon, but they didn't ask me any questions. They were waiting for me to leave and wouldn't be at all pleased to find the car locked up.

I crossed the plaza slowly, looking at the gray houses that probably had long yards and gardens behind them. A drunk was passing by on horseback, smashing bottles against the walls. The noise gave me a stupid, almost infantile scare, and I hid behind a tree. The hick was shouting, "Communism is finished, god-damn it!," laughing as he made his way down the town's only street, which led to the country. The police hadn't budged from the shop, where the light was still on. When things were quiet again, I crossed the street and walked into the front hall of the boardinghouse.

Lem had taken one of the rooms that looked out onto a square patio paved with flagstones. It was so dark that I felt my way along with a broomstick, and before entering the room, I knocked and asked permission. I needed that peculiar man I didn't know, who had appeared out of thin air. When I went in, I found him pacing with a whiskey in one hand and a cigarette in the other. He was in his underpants, but he'd forgotten to take off his jacket, and that gave him a ridiculous, slightly desolate air.

"There's no telephone in this dump," he announced, making a gesture of disgust while staring at the paint peeling off the ceiling stained by twenty or thirty years of cigarette smoke. The plaster on the walls was cracked, and tiny weeds were poking their way through the bricks. A long line of ants was parading under the door carrying bits of leaves and, occasionally, a petal fallen from the vases out in the patio. The window was open, but it was still possible to smell the rancid stink of the mattresses.

"At least it's got a roof," I said.

"What do you say we get something to eat? I'm tired of eating junk."

"Eat? Where do you think we are, Copacabana?"

"There has to be a restaurant. A place where we can order a hamburger."

"No restaurant, no casino. Forget it."

He became sad, as if I had let him down. He couldn't have been more than fifty years old, but his hair was as dry as a bush languishing at the side of the road. He was wearing wool socks and shoes that were color-coordinated with his car.

"Might there be ice?"

"Didn't you ask the owner?"

"He was sleepy, and I didn't want to bother him."

I sat down on one of the beds, and the noise of the springs was music to my ears. I took off my jacket, but since I wasn't wearing underpants, I had to keep my trousers on. The sheets were blue and almost clean.

"I brought a little chocolate from the car," I said, pointing to my bag.

He made a fatigued face, wiped his mouth with his handkerchief, and insisted politely:

"Wouldn't you like to walk a little? Who knows, something might be open."

"I already checked; everything's closed."

"You give up right away, eh? If you don't mind then . . ." He pointed to my bag, which was on the table.

"Please help yourself," I answered, and I watched him look through my belongings until he found the notebook and his eyes lit up. He put it on the night table, opened the chocolate, and offered me my share.

"I wanted to talk to you about this." He showed me the notebook and sat down on the other bed. He paused as if he were about to begin explaining, and had suddenly forgotten what he was going to say. He stared at my bandage and asked if I'd had any problems with the police.

"None that I know of."

"Is what you told me back there true?"

"What?" I asked, although I knew what was coming.

"That you know about computers."

"I told you then that computers are useless for roulette. Everybody's tried it, and it's no use, it doesn't work."

"You're a pessimist, it's written all over your face."

"I've heard it all before, that's all."

"An incurable pessimist," he said to himself, smoothing out his hair. "Mind if I ask what happened to your leg?"

"A dog bit me."

"Now I understand! A thing like that can depress you. Look, I'm not asking much. I've got a blank space here"—he pointed to a page in the notebook—"and I need to study the matter a little. But I have no head for numbers. I'm getting old."

"You already told me that. What do you say we get some sleep?"

"Sorry, I didn't want to bother you."

When he got into bed, he realized he had his jacket on and got up to take it off. There was no closet, and after hesitating a moment, he hung it on the back of the chair, on top of mine.

"You could have taken off with the car," he said in passing, as he got back into bed.

"Think I would have gotten far?"

"Why not? I got to Alaska."

He remained quiet, staring at the ceiling. He forgot me, and he forgot to turn off the light. I got up, took off the bandage, and went to wash out the wound, which was quite swollen. While I dried myself off, I looked through my jacket pocket. Lem was in another world, and wherever that was, he was having a rough time. I found the half-smoked, lipstick-stained cigarette and put it on the night table next to the clock. I got into bed without making any noise, put out the night-light, and instantly fell asleep.

8   It wasn't yet 6 a.m. when I was jolted awake by some cows mooing outside the window. I felt the same fear when I was sleeping out in the open and dreamed the cows were about to trample me. Lem was still in bed, but when I got up later, at 9:30, he'd already gone. Not a trace remained of him: not the car key, not the whiskey bottle, not even the lipstick-stained cigarette. I looked through my bag and didn't find the revolver, either. I prayed he'd paid the bill and hastily washed up with the dirty, dried-out soap.

I left my bag in the room and went out into the hall where I ran into the owner, who was wearing baggy black gaucho-style trousers. He wanted to know if we'd had a good night's sleep and asked for my identification card so he could write my name down in the register. He told me Lem had left early, asking him to give me the change from the bill. I took the money without counting it and went to have a look at the bar on the corner. The sidewalk was covered in places with dry thistles that caught onto my trousers. The bar had a long counter and a few tables where customers were playing cards or dice. In the back, I could see a grill and a private room as well. I sat down. On the wall were two posters: one announced a *truco* competition, and the other the visit of Nadia, Doctor of Law, Fortune-teller, and Astrologer.

I ordered coffee and asked what they might have to go along with it. I was served a homemade biscuit, which I smothered with butter and *dulce de leche*. I calculated that with the heap of money I had in my pocket, I'd have enough for a good breakfast. I had another coffee while the customers, elbows on the counter, watched me out of the corner of their eyes. My leg felt fine, and I told myself that Lem had behaved like a gentleman even if I had disappointed him. Now I could walk again or stay there until I was picked up by another car. I saw a Rastrojero go by carrying a tied-up hog and then a Dodge Polara without a hood. On the other side of the plaza there was an office with the flag hanging outside it, and I concluded it must be either the municipal government or the post office. The Ford Falcon that belonged to the police was parked in the shade of some trees. A boy who came out of the private room offered to shine my shoes and asked me if I'd ever been to Italpark and if it was true that the people in Buenos Aires had eaten the animals in the zoo. I began to laugh, but he told me he'd heard it on the radio, so I decided to believe him so he wouldn't carry on. All the customers were still staring at me, and I began to feel annoyed. On the corner of the plaza there was a tall monolith, similar to the one in Colonia Vela, and I asked the boy if he knew anything about the soldier.

"He was a leather tanner from El Remanso," he proudly told me, as if El Remanso were the most famous place in the country.

"Is there an army base near here?"

"No. If you're from Triunvirato, you do your conscription time in Tandil. I've got—" He counted the years on his fingers and reached seven. He had a problem pronouncing "conscription" so he switched to "service" to go on with the conversation. Finally, and I think he started talking to me for that reason only, he wanted to know what I did for a living. I told him I was a medical inspector, but I was instantly sorry, because I could see in his eyes that in those parts they had no idea what that was.

"I'm on my way to Tandil," I said, to settle his mind. Then I gave him a tip.

I had more money than I thought. I called the owner over, paid him, and told myself it would be a good idea to change my trousers. At the same time, I could buy underpants and sandals so walking would be more comfortable. A very blond, sweaty man with a sheep dog walked into the bar shouting that it would rain that night, but the news didn't make anyone put down his glass of red wine. The conversation was like a uniform noise from which a burst of laughter would jump out from time to time. I got up slowly so I wouldn't attract attention and walked out to the sidewalk. For the first time, I saw women passing by with their purchases. I went to the building where the flag was flying and stopped outside; a crowd was beginning to gather silently, waiting to be fed. There were old people dressed up in their best clothes, and field hands who obeyed every order given by a woman who worked there. I asked her if she'd seen a man in a suit who might have come to use the telephone. At first she said no, but I persisted and she answered that perhaps, that it might have happened that the man could have come when she was helping the postman. All the same, she pointed out, the telephone was out of order because the sun had dried out the wires or something like that. Since she was scowling at me, I inquired as to where I might find a store, and a farmhand told me to walk to the next corner. I went out, passed by police headquarters, which was a big house with bars on the windows, and crossed toward the repair shop where I'd left the Jaguar.

Two boys who looked like brothers were working on a motor suspended on two chains. The kid who'd taken care of me the previous night stood up, went to the workbench, and handed me a wrinkled envelope.

"The other gentleman left this for you."

"What time did he come by?"

"He was already waiting when we opened up."

"He didn't leave any message?"

"No. Just the envelope, nothing else."

I opened it on the street and found the red notebook, inside of which was a card with Lem's name engraved on it. "Why don't you try it?" was written on it in a trembling hand, perhaps because he'd written it standing up. On the other side, he'd written "Send me word," and nothing else.

I walked to the store without taking my eyes off the hungry-looking dogs wandering around in packs. I had the sensation that an invisible, nocturnal earthquake had taken place, something that had swallowed up the people's soul. Perhaps I was beginning to feel alone again and nothing more, but I couldn't shake off the impression that something was taking shape that would change everything.

The store had a meager stock. I found a pair of white underpants in my size and picked out a pair of work pants they had to hem. I also bought two wash-and-wear shirts, but when I tried to pay, the owner told me to come back that afternoon because prices changed so much he didn't know how much he'd have to charge me. At least I was able to take the underpants with me. I returned to the boardinghouse before they closed down for the siesta. I told the owner I'd be staying another night, and he told me it was okay as long as I didn't want the room Lem and I had shared, because he'd just rented it to a lady who told fortunes. The vacant room, he said, was cheaper, because the glass had been stolen from the window.

9 I slid the table over in front of the window and began to study Lem's notebook. The handwriting was easier to read than it was on the card. From time to time an undecipherable commentary would slip in, but someone had carried out the colossal task of noting which numbers had come up at the roulette tables over the course of a year. I instantly saw how he'd hit the ceiling when the ball, after landing on random numbers during its first two dozen rolls, had suddenly landed in the last slot.

I read carefully until I thought I'd discovered a certain logic in the reappearance of 17 after the house moved the wheels to different tables. Something similar happened with 21, which won several times in a short period and then disappeared. If I'd been able to check a few books, things would have been easier, but in any case I had nothing else to do, and the idea of refreshing my memory with some algebra comforted me a bit. I asked the owner of the boardinghouse for a pencil and a coffee before he went to sleep. He returned my identification card and asked me if I wanted a turn with Madame Nadia, who would begin to see people after the siesta. I said no and asked permission to make myself a Nescafé.

I found his wife in the kitchen. With an accent I couldn't quite place, she evoked the elegance of the blond young man who'd come with me. I told her Lem had gray hair and was middle-aged, but for her he went right on being as blond as Robert Redford. Since I wanted to get back to my calculations, I conceded the point and asked her for some cookies to have with the coffee.

Back in the room, I tore some blank pages out of the notebook and sat down in the light coming through the window. The person who'd stolen the glass had done an impeccable job of removing the dry putty with a penknife. I imagined him standing on top of the bed at dawn, sliding out the two panes, being careful not to cut his fingers. They couldn't have been worth much, but the thief would have said it was better than nothing.

For a couple of hours, I forgot everything. I wrote from memory, as diligently as I had when I worked in the institute. Except that I didn't have a computer, which I would eventually need to make the program work. Every time I looked up, the line of people waiting to see Madame Nadia was longer. By 4 p.m., the whole town was there, even the two brothers from the repair shop and a few farmworkers I'd seen in the bar. All of them wanted to know what the future had in store for them. The fortune-teller worked with the door closed. Her room was opposite my window, so whenever one client left and another entered, I'd catch a glimpse of her sitting behind a big table she'd borrowed from the owner of the boardinghouse.

At sundown, when I went over to the store to pick up my trousers, the police car pulled up at the boardinghouse door and waited until she came out with her purse and left everyone cooling their heels until seven o'clock. During all that time, no one left his place in line. It was a gathering of neighbors, more women than men, and everyone brought something to give her: chickens, cakes, sausages, salami, and other things whose use I couldn't figure out. Even a guitar player appeared, but he couldn't manage to get anyone's attention and left. Later on, they threw out a grumbling drunk who'd come to complain about an unfulfilled promise.

At first the townspeople would saunter over to my window in a phony, nonchalant way, but later on they came in groups, as if amused to see me working over a sheet of paper. One even dared to ask me for a cigarette, but later there were so many who asked that I had to hide the pack. I was struggling with the algebra when Nadia, Doctor of Law, returned with a huge package that smelled like roast suckling pig, and attention was once again focused on the room next door. The line formed again with no arguments, and by dinner hour only three or four women were still waiting. Almost everyone came out smiling except two young women who went their way crying, but without making a scene. The Lawyer hadn't made much money, but she'd be driving away with a carload of provisions. For an instant I thought about Coluccini, who must have been getting nearer and nearer to his Bolivian dream, providing the Gordini held out. I looked at the sheets of paper covered with numbers and told myself that early the next morning I'd get back on the road. Lem had requested I get in touch with him, but he hadn't told me where or how, so I didn't feel I owed him anything in particular.

Having taken care of her last client, Nadia went out to the

patio, saw me sitting at the window, and acknowledged my greeting. She looked about forty-five years old, had bleached blond hair, and quite a few more pounds than she needed. She was wearing pleated trousers cut wide and a flowered blouse. When she went back to her room, she locked and bolted the door, no doubt so she could count her take. I put the notebook in my pocket, slid the table back to its regular place, and got ready to eat before they closed the bar. Since I had no desire to expose myself again to the locals' curiosity, I put on my new trousers, a blue shirt, and gave the owner's wife some money to wash and press my jacket. Too bad if she ruined it. On the way out, I again ran into the fortune-teller, who was hesitating outside the door to her room.

"Are you from around here, mister?" she asked me, although she only wanted to confirm I wasn't. I said no, and she told me she came from La Plata. It made her nervous to leave the room unguarded, with only that flimsy lock. I suggested she speak to the owner, but she made a disdainful gesture. Her eyebrows were jet black, and she had a beauty spot on one cheek. She didn't appear to have a very high opinion of her fellow man.

"I'm going out to eat, but I'll be right back," I said. "Wait until I get back, and then you can go out without worrying."

She studied me awhile but didn't have enough light to read my eyes.

"The police chief told me that at ten o'clock he was going to send over a patrolman," she said. "Would you like to eat something here? I mean, if you aren't meeting anyone."

I didn't know if the part about the guard was true or if it were some trick to set a limit on the evening. The idea that the whole town would gather to watch me eat in a corner of the bar wasn't exactly my idea of fun, so I decided to join her.

"It would be my pleasure," I said.

We went to her room, she pointed to a chair for me, and left the door ajar so no one would get the wrong idea. It was like a delicatessen: on the floor, on top of both beds, and inside the lavatory were homemade empanadas, salami, cheeses, wine, cakes, and even two cans of motor oil. She put some silverware on the table, gave me a bottle of red wine to open, and told me to take whatever I liked. I chose a couple of empanadas and a piece of cheese, while she got out two paper cups, for which she apologized, saying she didn't usually have guests. That made her laugh, as if she were making fun of herself. On the table were two packs of well-thumbed cards, a candle burned half-way down, and the stubs of the others she'd used during the afternoon. We ate with gusto, making small talk, and when she found out I worked with computers, she made a gesture of horror.

"Now they're doing astrology by computer. Did you know that?"

"Do you go out on tour much?" I asked.

"People are nicer in the interior," she answered. "More honest."

"Then why are you worried about the room?"

I didn't mean to annoy her, but she didn't like the question.

"There's always someone around who's in love with other people's property," she defended herself, as she took a sip of wine with affected delicacy. Then she sorted through the desserts on the bed and chose a lemon cake. She cut two big pieces, picked up the cards in one hand and, as she ate, shuffled them with the skill of a professional. She'd hung an astrological chart on the wall to impress her clientele.

"How can you work without a cat?" I asked her, and then she opened her eyes as wide as plums. Under her bleached hair, she had the head of a gypsy, rather battered by time. She must have kept a pistol hidden somewhere, like Lem.

"Are you in the business?" she asked.

"No, but I've been told that without a cat it's impossible to do anything."

She smiled. Under her blouse, she had opulent breasts that were still firm. Even though the light was bad, I could see the wrinkles on her neck. Suddenly, out of the pack she was shuffling with one hand, there emerged a single card that fell right in the center of the table. A king of clubs.

"Excuse me," she said, "I have to know something about you."

"All you have to do is ask," I told her, but she wasn't listening to me. She cut herself another piece of cake and poured herself some more wine as a four of hearts fell on top of the king.

"Been separated long?"

"A year or two, I don't know."

"You've got a son or daughter far away. I'm asking you if you've been alone for a long time."

"Can't you find out without my help?"

"I don't have the cat," she said mockingly, as she ran her tongue over her lips to pick up a bit of lemon. "You used to live far away. Political problems, right? You might be an engineer, but things aren't going well."

"You don't need cards to figure that out."

"Why did you come back? You had a good job there. Someone very important back there who relied on you."

She laid out four cards face down and told me to turn them over in any order I chose. The game interested and humiliated me at the same time.

"Italy, France, a city where your child is. Male or female, I can't see clearly."

"Female."

"In Spain," she said. "She writes constantly, and you don't answer."

She looked up to see what effect that would have on me. I felt like talking to her about calculating probabilities, but I figured she probably had a car and that it would be terrific if she'd get me to the highway.

"What are you doing around here?" I asked. "Not enough business in La Plata?"

"Competition's heavy. Before, my husband would cover the north and I would take care of the south, but now I do it all myself. By next month, we'll be living in Brazil. The kids are already there."

I looked at the provisions she'd been given and pointed out that if she weren't paid with money it was going to be hard to make the trip.

"Don't believe that for a minute. All this comes in handy. Don't you want to know if your daughter's all right?"

"Do you know?"

She shuffled the cards like a real card sharp and asked me to pick two.

"The kid's okay. Maybe even someone's girlfriend. You didn't make life easy for her."

"Could I have done otherwise?"

She shrugged her shoulders and then shook her yellow mop of hair. I asked if it would bother her if I smoked, and she answered no with a gesture.

"You're not going anywhere," she said.

She really liked the lemon cake and was going to eat the whole thing. With each piece she cut, her eyes glittered in a different way. She was escaping the sadness of always talking about other people.

"What's your astrological sign?" she insisted.

"What difference does it make? I've made up several astrological programs myself."

"Know something? Don't get angry now, but you're tired of putting up with yourself."

We stared at each other for a moment. Maybe she was talking about herself, but she'd still managed to hurt me.

I suddenly thought a cat had passed in front of the door, but it was the patrolman arriving.

"Two girls left in tears this afternoon. Was that necessary?"

"I can't give good news to everyone. No one would believe me."

"You think you know who I am?"

"Better than you do. Where do you want me to drop you tomorrow?"

"Anywhere. A man gave me a job to do, but he had to leave in a hurry."

She looked around her at the filthy walls covered with cobwebs.

"He wants to break the bank at a casino," I added.

She ate the last crumbs off the cake dish, put the deck on the table, and pulled out a card with a fingernail that was so sharp it looked like a scalpel.

"A faceless man in a bad way," she read somewhere.

I said that was the case.

"Finish the job. It's his last chance."

10 Just as Nadia turned out the light, the deluge predicted by the blond man in the bar broke loose. The sky suddenly closed up, and the storm began with a prelude of thunder and lightning before the rains came. Water poured through the window right onto the bed, which I instantly moved so I'd be able to sleep. I set about checking what I'd written, looking for errors and adding numbers, when I remembered the patrolman, a dark-haired little man in a uniform that obviously belonged to a much larger man. Wrapped in a towel, I stuck my head out of the window and saw him leaning against the wall, soaked to the skin, his cap pulled down to his ears. The owner of the boardinghouse had closed up the hallway to keep it from flooding, and everyone had forgotten about the patrolman standing guard. I opened the door and shouted to him over the noise of the storm. The poor bastard came over without even trying to protect himself, taking his job seriously; he snapped to attention at the door, his open hand against the visor of his cap.

"Officer Benítez at your orders," he said, standing there in hope that someone would tell him what this was all about. His web belt was so old and tattered that his pistol looked as if it would fall out at any moment. Under his jacket, he was carrying some old Spanish magazines Nadia had given him to amuse himself while on guard.

"Come on in, man, you're going to catch cold out there," I said, but he stayed right where he was, under the rain. I was in my underpants, and the gusts of rain made me jump back.

"But sir, I'm standing guard," he said. "Until four, I'm on duty."

"Stand guard inside," I shouted to him. Tiny droplets slid off his visor. The number on the badge he wore on his chest ended in "21," a number Lem was searching for and one I'd worked on all afternoon. He hesitated a moment, looked behind himself, took off his cap, and walked in happily.

"Thanks, sir. A drink would sure come in handy."

I closed the door and told him I had nothing to give him but a cigarette. Disillusioned, he stared at me for a while, his uniform dripping onto the floor, his big shoes pointing to the corners of the wall.

"You're the gentleman with the car," he said, making a gesture of admiration.

"Sit down," I said, handing him the towel.

"They ripped off the window," he observed. "Why didn't you ask for some plastic bags to cover the hole?"

He aspirated his *s*'s and swallowed a few other letters to speak more quickly. I insisted he sit down and told him I was going to try to get some sleep. He hung his cap on the back of the chair, said the rain was good for the crops, and began to leaf through the magazines, although from time to time he looked at me, wanting to chat. I finished checking over the program, put away the notebook, and wrapped myself in the sheet. The patrolman asked me if he had to turn out the light, and I answered no, that he could read in peace. He seemed fascinated by the color illustrations and stared for a long time at the photos of some Spanish yuppie playing tennis and sunning himself next to a pool. He forgot about me: he began to nod and fell asleep before I did.

It must have been 3 a.m. when Nadia began shouting, first an anguished howl and then two or three whimpers that seemed to come from beyond the grave. Benítez jumped to his feet, took out his flashlight, and grabbed his pistol, all with the face of a man who's lost his job. While I pulled on my trousers, I looked through the window, but I saw nothing strange. The patrolman went out into the storm, carrying the same broomstick in front of him that I'd used to feel my way in the dark, and kicked Nadia's door without a second thought, just like cops on television. I went out after him, cursing because my new trousers were getting wet, but the door didn't give, and we just stood there in the rain, staring at each other like a pair of idiots.

The only light came from our room and from the lightning. When Nadia shouted again, Benítez looked at me as if I were his boss, and stepped back to make another charge at the door. He wasn't big enough for the job, and I had to help him a bit. Finally the lock broke and we stumbled in, tripping over cheeses and empanadas. Nadia was in her slip, sitting on the bed, and around her were a couple of empty wine bottles and a bottle of gin which had spilled onto the sheets. Her eyes were rolled back, and with a ring-covered finger she pointed behind us. "There! there!" she repeated to herself. She didn't look like someone on her way to Brazil. Benítez turned around with his flashlight, but only found the wall with the astrological chart. Nadia held out her hands, but it wasn't the two of us she was begging. I told Benítez to calm down, that it was just a nightmare, but he didn't listen to me, and went to look under the bed, where he found an empty suitcase.

"No, sir, I think the medium here is drunk," he said, and I could see he was an expert in pointing out irrefutable facts. He picked up the empty bottles, lined them up against the wall, and told me he'd have to report the incident. I went and sat down next to Nadia, who touched my face like a sleepwalker. I took a cigarette from the pack on the night table, lit it for her, and put it between her lips. By pure reflex action, she inhaled; it made her choke, and she became upset again.

I tried to make her lie down on her side, although at first she fought back, and then she began to shake from head to toe. In the struggle, a breast escaped from the slip and revealed its somewhat withered glory to us. The nipple had a huge violet halo around it, or it may have been the half-light that fooled me. I let Benítez take a look and then straightened her clothes. As soon as she'd calmed down, I removed some jars of candy and a few hams so I could get the blanket off the floor. I covered her up and looked around for something that would make her vomit. Benítez said it was best to put drunks face down, assuring me that he had experience in these things. I went out to find a basin while he prepared a mixture of maté, quince jelly, and God knows what else. I hadn't heard thunder like that for some time and thought the storm had worsened the effects of the alcohol. Beyond the wall enclosing the patio, the horizon was sealed tight, and no one else seemed awake. I emptied the basin and went back to the room.

"My relief should be getting here just about now," Benítez said, stirring the mixture in a glass. I concluded he wouldn't want another member of the force to see him in an awkward situation, so I brought the basin over to the bedside. Then, when he signaled he was ready, I raised her head and pinched her nostrils shut. She didn't need more than two sips to put her head down and throw up everything she had. Benítez smiled, satisfied, even though Nadia insulted us and demanded we call the police. As soon as she let me come close to her again, I combed her hair a bit, put a sweater over her shoulders, and took away the basin. After a while, I saw she was fixing herself up on her own, so I went back to my room, but Benítez stayed behind, carrying out his orders under the downpour.

The other patrolman came half an hour late. I thought Nadia would sleep all day, that with the storm it would be impossible to leave town, and I decided to go on foot as soon as the rain stopped. I wrapped myself up in the sheet, even my head, because gusts of wind would occasionally blast into the room. I fell asleep before sunrise.

I was in a deep sleep when I heard Nadia's voice through the empty window. I woke up, surprised. The wind bent her hat back, and she smiled at me through fresh lipstick. She'd put on sunglasses and a raincoat even though the rain had subsided. She'd just done her nails and had all her rings on.

"Come on, help me load up the stuff," she said, with disconcerting optimism. I told her to wait until I dressed, and when I got up, I saw it was ten o'clock. My new things were still wet, so I had to put on my torn trousers and a different shirt. Then I went to pick up the jacket the woman from the boardinghouse had pressed for me. The street was as muddy and full of puddles as a barnyard, and I thought no car would be able to make it through, but Nadia appeared at the wheel of an ancient Deux Chevaux which somehow managed to move forward.

"Well?" she shouted to me as she backed in. "Like to spend another night in this paradise?"

I went back to the room and wrote a message for Lem on the wall. I told him I was preparing what he'd asked for and that now I was on my way to La Plata.

11   It took the patrolman and me ten trips to empty Nadia's room. She just stood there in her ankle-length raincoat giving us orders. She seemed used to it and knew how to use every corner of the car. When the Citroën was completely packed, she told me the weight made the car ride better and passed me a thermos of coffee the boardinghouse people had made for her. Before leaving, she gave a few cans of pâté de foie gras to the patrolman and said good-bye to everyone, just like a campaigning politician. As soon as she pulled onto the town's

only street, I realized she had the same problem as Coluccini: she couldn't shift into high, and the car would swerve and lose speed. The windshield wipers looked like toys, and since the one on her side didn't work, she had to lean over to my side to see where she was going. The Citroën skidded sideways more than once until we finally hit the main road and Nadia kept two wheels right in the tracks of a tractor, which steadied the car nicely. The chassis may have sounded like a bunch of tin cans being dragged along on a string, but we were leaving Triunvirato, and that made both of us happy. I opened the thermos to give her some coffee, but she said a shot of gin would suit her better.

"You were pretty mad last night when you left," she suddenly reprimanded me.

"I'm sorry, I just didn't realize it," I answered in confusion as I poured a shot into a glass. She gestured for me to put in a little more. We were doing about twenty miles per hour, but it seemed like more than sixty.

"Don't worry." An understanding smile appeared behind her sunglasses. "Men really suffer when they travel alone. Bengochea would always be a wreck when he got home."

"Did he do astrology too?"

"Astrology, encyclopedias, toys, all depending on the place."

"You must not see much of each other."

She looked at me in surprise.

"As much as I care to," she said. "Every time I leave, I wonder if I'm coming back. Later, the cards say I will, that he's better than nothing; so here I am, on the way home. Bengochea's seductive, eh?, he's got his charms."

"I understand."

"I really don't know if you men do understand. Women have a different sensibility. We've always got to put up with something brutal. From our husbands or from some other man. Do you understand that?"

"I think so."

She didn't seem convinced. She swerved around a rock,

bounced off the edge of a hole, and asked me if I'd eaten breakfast.

"No, I didn't have time."

"Then make yourself a sandwich. That's all I eat when I'm working."

"Are we far from the highway?"

"A couple of hours, more or less. Where are you going?"

"Nowhere . . . That's what you told me last night."

"Did you have a session with me yesterday?"

"We ate dinner together in your room."

She searched through her handbag, took out the cards, and while she held the wheel steady with one hand, shuffled with the other. Finally she tossed a six of clubs onto her skirt, immediately followed by an ace of diamonds.

"I had to throw you out because you were drunk and starting to become a nuisance."

"Sorry," I said.

She dealt a couple of other cards and looked at them out of the corner of her eye, always leaning over to my side to watch the deserted road. The clouds were hanging lower and lower, heavier and heavier with rain.

"There are sorrows in your life. . . . But who doesn't have them?"

"What do the cards tell you?" I asked.

She shrugged and put on her glasses.

"A far-away country. Bengochea's going to die soon. The kids will get married. . . . Nothing exceptional."

"Want me to make you a sandwich?"

"Ham with a little mayonnaise, please. You'll find everything in the shoe box."

I sliced some feta cheese and put it on the bread, which was very moist. The windows of the car were clouded over; it didn't matter because there was nothing to see. It was as if we were standing still. As I spread the mayonnaise, Nadia swerved to ford a pond that had formed in a hollow. At first, the Citroën stayed on course, clinging to the bottom of the swamp, but the waves we made rolled back and pushed us all over the place. Nadia twisted the wheel a few times, but it was useless: the water carried us away like a paper boat.

The car floated awhile, then slammed against a hummock, and I landed on top of Nadia because there was nothing for me to hold on to. All our baggage also moved in the same direction, and the car drifted twenty or thirty yards before it came to a stop against the wire fence. Muddy water began to seep in through the floor, carrying away our sandwiches and covering our feet. The motor went on working for a few more minutes, but when the water covered the exhaust pipe, it stalled with a muffled backfire.

Nadia insulted all the gods, punched the wheel several times, and then took off her glasses, which were spattered with mud. She was the desolate shadow of the woman I'd seen during the night; her eyes were red, and the gray roots of her hair were showing through. She looked like the captain of a pirate ship at the mercy of a storm. The sausages and canned goods began to float around us, and I realized she'd accepted defeat. Without saying a word, she opened her window, looked at the flood, sat back in her seat, and took out her compact. We floated along, and the rain came down harder, as if it were there for all eternity. Nadia looked into her mirror and put on lipstick with all the care of a teenager.

"Don't be frightened," she said. "Make the sandwiches, and let's eat in peace."

I sorted through the wet box, but most of the provisions had been scattered by the flood.

"You really don't remember?" I asked.

"What should I remember?"

"Nothing."

I had to dry the ham with a rag. The mayonnaise jar was lost under the seat, but the bread was safe because it had been caught between two cans of oil. We drank a bottle of very light white wine and then opened a bottle of red that was much better.

"Bengochea's got a really pretty girlfriend," Nadia informed me. She took out a billfold and passed me her husband's photo. He was thin and bald and wore thick glasses and a suit he'd bought in the Jewish section of Buenos Aires.

"She turned up in the cards, but I didn't say anything to him because I know the poor man doesn't have much time left. You can probably imagine we haven't slept together for a long time, but what intrigued me about all this was how he could have conquered her. One day, I had him followed by one of those private detectives on Avenida de Mayo who put ads in the newspaper. He made me pay in dollars, the crook, but to give the devil his due, he caught them right away."

"Who was she?"

"She worked in a toy store. At the time, he worked on the bus, selling dolls he bought from a wholesaler. We were paying off the TV set, I remember. So I went to see the little snot and asked her what she saw in Bengochea. At the beginning, of course, she cried, but later we went to a café, and she told me he was a very tender man, very mannerly, that he gave her flowers and little presents. Is that how he looks to you?"

She showed me his photo again. He looked like a guy who'd get lost walking out the front door. Then she passed me a photo of the girl, a little blonde smiling with Palermo Park lake in Buenos Aires behind her.

"How did you get this picture?"

"She gave it to me. We went to the movies, and then she came home with me so I could read the cards for her. When Bengochea turned up, he almost dropped dead. From now on, I said to the two of them, I want you to see each other here at home, in front of me."

She looked at me to see what I thought.

"What about the kids?"

"They were already in Brazil. They have a rock band."

"What did Bengochea say?"

"His back went up. 'I'm going to live with her,' he told me."

"He made up his mind."

"Not really. I gave both of them a slap, and that was the end of that."

"You mean they stopped seeing each other?"

"No, they see each other at home, in the living room. Sometimes the three of us go to the movies together. She's like our daughter. Someday she'll find another boyfriend and get married."

"Why are you telling me all this?"

"I don't know. We're locked in here, and you tell me that last night I invited you to have dinner with me."

I looked at her as she cleared a space in the Citroën. The only dry place left was the seats, so we'd have to make do with them. She smiled at me so tenderly I couldn't stop myself: I took her by the shoulders and kissed near the mouth. She searched for me with her freshly rouged lips, with her fat, thick tongue, and we slowly positioned ourselves. The car was rocking under the rain, but I wanted to see those big, violet-tipped breasts again. The zipper on her blouse, however, wouldn't open, and I had to grab on to the shift lever so I wouldn't fall. Nadia stretched her leg along the backrest and let me keep going but without helping in any way. There was no way to get rid of the skirt, but when she put her arms around my neck, her blouse opened, and I felt a smooth softness that filled my hands. I must have groaned or maybe I said something, because she squeezed me against her lips and wouldn't let me slide my head down until much later, after she'd undone my trousers and was sure everything would go well.

Without any warning, I was on my back with the steering wheel touching my nose and one arm in the water. Nadia had to pull one leg free to bring her mouth to mine. She gave me a long, hard kiss with one knee against mine and the other on the littered floor. I wanted to touch her nipples, enjoy looking at them after not having made love for such a long time, and I took hold of her waist to break the kiss. Suddenly she raised up, and I saw the cascade that came out between the folds of her blouse.

I rested my head against the window and managed to give her a little bite on that white skin. Nadia jumped and hit the ceiling, but I don't think it mattered much to her. We stayed like that for a long time: I was breathing hard through my nose because the weight of her body pressed me against the window, and she was panting a little, not faking but sincere, with her eyes closed and her tongue between her teeth.

There wasn't a trace of lipstick on her lips, which were now two fine, tremulous lines. One of my arms was pinned down, but I slipped the other under her skirt and pulled the wet elastic. If we could have stood up or changed position, things would have been easy, but we were inside a bubble and doing the best we could. She managed to get the skirt out of the way while I pulled down my trousers and caressed her breasts. I shifted around to get into position, and she pulled off her stockings and panties, all in a feverish nervousness, until she grabbed hold of me around the waist and we were left breathless. I softly felt for her, and she pressed herself close to me carefully, the way you slip on a glove. She offered me her lips, and for a second both of us kept perfectly still. The shadows under her eyes had disappeared, and she looked as if her mind was miles away. I too visited some good memories. I was afraid of my own pathetic cries, and when Nadia pulled herself away from me, clenching a fist and panting, I realized that for a long time I'd forgotten myself, which meant that I couldn't help anyone else.

She slumped to the side and looked at me for an instant, wanting to say something. But she didn't. I thought it was better that way: maybe she was thinking about Bengochea or Brazil or about me and what she'd seen in the cards, which were now floating near the Citroën's pedals. We hadn't been able to take off our clothes, and we silently set about putting ourselves back together, each leaning against a door. We were filthy and our hair unkempt, and we had to save what things we could from the water. I wiped my hand over the windshield and through the fog managed to see both trees and telephone poles. Nadia passed me some chocolate cake and confessed she'd never studied astrology, that she owed her skill with the cards to a Catalan teacher she'd had an affair with when she was very young. She never spoke familiarly to me; she maintained a warm distance, and I noticed that without thinking of it, she'd already excluded me from any intimacy with her.

I held out as long as I could, but when afternoon came, I had to get out of the car to find a private place. I rolled up my trousers and walked toward the trees. I found solid ground there and some bushes that smelled like mint. I urinated and then stretched my legs. In the distance, following the same route we'd taken, I seemed to see a flutter of big birds and the splatter of mud flying up against the rain. The din came closer and closer, and I could hear a motor going at top speed. I was afraid whoever it was wouldn't see the Citroën floating in the swamp, so I ran to flag them down. Then I saw Lem's Jaguar rocking between the puddles, frenetic, as if it were chasing something that would inevitably escape.

12 Lem saw me right away, and once he'd crossed the swamp, he began to slow down. I ran to meet him, happy I wouldn't have to spend the whole night there, ready to play along with him as far as he'd care to go. As soon as he got out, I realized things hadn't gone his way. I shouted to Nadia that it was my friend and waited to see if he'd wet his feet to come and meet me. He didn't. He stood on a rise waiting for me, and as I got closer I began to remember some of his facial features. He'd changed his clothes; even his tie was new. As soon as I got close to him, he threw himself on top of me, grabbed my neck, and squeezed with all his might while he kicked me in the shins.

He took me by surprise and almost strangled me because he

had long, solid fingers and I was off-guard. I managed to push his face with one hand to get him off me, and when I convinced myself it was no joke, I returned him a few kicks in the shins. Then he insulted me, but without much conviction. He actually seemed disappointed. He couldn't choke me, so he tried to punch me, but I ducked to avoid his fists and smashed my elbow into his stomach. Neither of us knew very much about fighting, and we were wrestling and exchanging slaps that were more awkward than painful. It didn't bother me to go back to the water, but he tried to keep his distance because he was wearing dry clothes. He had even put on cologne.

Nadia shouted something to me, but I didn't understand because my ears were ringing. She seemed to be coming to help me, so I motioned to her not to budge. Lem took advantage of my distraction to punch me hard in the back of the neck, and I suddenly found myself sitting in the water. Then he bent over to talk to me.

"You could have told me you knew her, you piece of trash. What do you take me for?"

It was then I understood that I shouldn't have left the cigarette with lipstick on the night table back in Triunvirato without explaining how I got it. Sitting in the puddle, with the mud up to my waist, I remembered that even in high school I'd never been a good fighter. I tried to calm down and was relieved to see that Lem wasn't going to turn his victory into a glorious triumph. He only seemed a bit surprised at his own strength and asked for an explanation.

"Where do you know her from, eh? Where?"

Then I saw that Nadia was slowly walking over, half hidden, somewhat out of the picture. She'd rolled up her skirt and had a pullover draped over her shoulders. I decided to give her time to get over to us and told Lem I didn't know what he was talking about and that he could go to hell. That fired him up a little, but he didn't want to go on fighting. He asked me if I'd met her before or after he had. If it was before, it didn't matter; if it was after, it was my fault she stayed in Colonia Vela. He was explaining that to me, ready to break off our friendship, when Nadia came up out of the water onto the slope. Lem noticed her presence and stood up to greet her, expecting she was going to ask him something. Instead she slapped him so hard, he lost his balance. Nadia had her hair tied back and had put on fresh lipstick. She shouted for me to get up, that we had to get the car out of there, and when Lem tried to offer an opinion, she slapped him again, tumbling him into the water. He landed next to me, still trying to block the blow with his arm. The condition of his suit filled me with regret. Before we got up, I tried to convince him I didn't even know his girlfriend's name.

"I picked up the cigarette on the road when she left, and that's it."

He made a gesture of disappointment and looked me up and down.

"A man like you picking up butts . . . ," he reproached me.

Nadia stared at us without understanding, and when Lem turned around to shake hands with me, she made a grimace of disgust. I wanted to go on being the offended party, so I pushed him away. Only then did he realize he was just as filthy as we were and turned to Nadia to ask to whom he had the pleasure of speaking. She showered him with insults and dared to tell him that either we all got out of there or no one got out. Lem was slow to understand because small things rolled off his back the way the water dripped off his suit. I forgot my anger and explained that we had to get the Citroën out of the swamp because people were expecting Nadia in La Plata.

"I wouldn't say expecting me . . . ," she said, wiping the mud off her arms.

Lem looked confused, but finally got out of the water with an indifference that seemed sincere.

"What do you say we get something to eat first?" he proposed. I'd heard that before, but Nadia had just met him and thought he was making fun of her.

"Sure. There must be a restaurant right around the corner."

Lem followed the movement of her arm, but since he found

nothing, he looked around to see if he could find any lights. He was not ready to give up just like that.

"There has to be someplace to eat," he said.

A cool breeze was beginning to blow, although the clouds were as heavy as before.

"I've got a rope," Nadia told him. "Bring the car over."

Lem was thinking about something else. I recalled that he had every sort of thing in the Jaguar, and I wondered if he had a blanket or something we could wrap up in during the night. I went with Nadia to get the rope, and on the way she asked me where I'd met him.

"On the road," I said. "He drove me to Triunvirato and then disappeared."

"He's the man who gave you that job to do?"

I said he was and reminded her she'd advised me to help him.

"A strange man. And I know a lot of people."

When she was in the car, she pulled out some dry cards and laid out four or five on the seat.

"No, he's not the man of my dreams," she predicted. "He's not the man of anybody's dreams. Watch out for him, because he can complicate your travel plans."

I assured her I'd be careful, and then we sorted through the food until we found the rope. The smell of roast pork aroused my appetite, but I didn't have the nerve to tell her in case she would think I was taking advantage. Night was already falling, and I walked back over to Lem, who lit a cigarette. The rope was short, and I asked him to bring the Jaguar over so I could tie it on.

"I hope you're not offended," he said from the rise, where he stood as stiff as a fence post. "Someone told my girlfriend some nonsense, so when I saw the cigarette . . . She leaves the same lipstick stains on all of them, see?"

"Go fuck yourself," I answered, and then went to see if the key was in the car. The revolver was still in its place and had six bullets in it. It was a brand-new Colt with a blue butt, and looked as if it had never been fired.

"You have to understand," insisted Lem (by now he was get-ting on my nerves), "how a great project, a new life, all goes up in smoke because some busybody tells her 'That man is an adventurer.' "

"Of course. Now come down here and help."

"It wasn't her husband, who's a nice person," he went on declaiming. "No. It was someone else, a mystifier, a psychoana-lyst, a sideshow con man."

Finally he did come down, thin, tall, and perplexed. I had the feeling he was trembling under his soaked clothing.

"Does the lady deal in groceries?" he asked me discreetly.

"The lady is a fortune-teller and an astrologer."

"She tells fortunes? Seriously?"

By now Nadia was with us, still with her skirt rolled up.

"Meaning not the slightest disrespect, madam," Lem asked her. "Have you been in Colonia Vela during the past few days?"

"Yesterday. I was there yesterday," said Nadia, turning away from him to hand me the rope.

13 I thought Lem was going to tie it around her neck, but instead he looked away and stood there staring at the ground. It seemed to me he was afraid of her, or perhaps the fatalism he'd reproached me for had taken control of him. The three of us managed to get the Citroën closer to solid ground. I got the Jaguar and backed it to the edge of the water, keeping one wheel on solid ground. I tied on the rope and told Lem to pull forward slowly, keeping the wheels straight. Nadia was on her way to the Citroën, and I asked her if anyone in Colonia Vela had spoken to her about him.

"I don't know, his face doesn't say anything to me."

"No one mentioned a man who comes from far away?"

"From far away? I don't remember. People have so many dramas . . . Unless he's the lost banker . . ."

"What's that?"

"A woman told me the story of a banker who came from far away and got lost out in the country."

"He was from Rio de Janeiro."

"No, I'd have remembered that. He was from the United States, I think."

"Did you tell the woman the man was an adventurer?"

"It's possible. It's a word I use quite a bit."

Just then, Lem started up his car, and Nadia ran to hers. In a second, the Citroën was out of the swamp. When she came back, she was wearing a wide, satisfied grin, but Lem looked like a wreck.

"I'd like to talk to you for a minute," he said, taking her by the arm.

Nadia suggested he have a seat in the Citroën and signaled me to leave them alone. It gave me a chance to look for dry clothing in the Jaguar, where I found two brand-new suits which I didn't dare touch. I took off my shirt, wrung it out completely, and turned on the heater to dry it out. I lit a cigarette and waited for them to finish. I could barely see them through the wet windows. She seemed to be convincing him of something. Then she took out the cards.

When he got out of the Citroën, Lem looked better. Pensive, he took a few steps and lit another cigarette, staring into the sunset. I would have liked to know what was going on in his mind, but I was sure he'd never tell me. He walked around the Jaguar two or three times, dirtying his shoes, and then silently got in. I thought he'd need to be alone, but he gestured for me to stay with him.

"Forgive me," he said, "I behaved like an idiot."

"All right. Where are you going now?"

"What about you?"

"Wherever you take me."

"Fine, but allow me to take you to dinner."

"I have never turned you down."

"That's what I like to hear. Invite the lady, if you like."

I went to the Citroën. My legs hurt a bit, but mostly I was hungry and coming down with a cold.

"What did he tell you?" I asked Nadia.

"That's a secret. Like the confessional."

"He wants us to have dinner with him."

"He's had every kind of bad thing happen to him. Let him do whatever he likes."

"You don't want to come with us?"

Smiling, she blew me a kiss from the palm of her hand.

"Forget about me."

That was the last thing she said to me. She handed me my bag and pulled away in second gear, sliding from side to side. The road was so straight and the terrain so flat that it took a long time for her to disappear. Lem had already changed his clothes and told me to pick out what I liked. I put on a white shirt and a roomy pair of trousers; contact with the dry fabric made me feel better. In the glove compartment, I found some aspirin and took two. Lem offered me the wheel, but I said no, that he'd know better than I how to find a restaurant. He smiled and drove the Jaguar into the same tracks Nadia had followed. After a while, we caught up to the Citroën, but we couldn't pass it until Lem found a more solid stretch of shoulder and made a rather risky maneuver. Before speeding away, he waved to Nadia as if she were already a memory.

In a short while, we reached a paved road filled with potholes, and Lem turned onto it with a swerve. For an entire hour we saw nothing and had no idea which way we were going. The map was undecipherable, and I was afraid we'd run out of gas. Sometimes the road would disappear, and Lem would have to lean close to the windshield to wind his way around the puddles. After nine, we came to a traffic circle overgrown with weeds and saw the lights of an Automobile Club motel.

"The world begins right there," said Lem, slowing down.

"Doesn't it frighten you?" I asked.

He gave me a sarcastic look, with a smile that wrinkled his cheeks.

"Suppose I ask you the same question?"

"I'd give you the same answer, Mister Lem."

He lowered his eyes for an instant, as if something I'd said upset him, and turned into the motel driveway. There was an old bus from the 152 line in Buenos Aires, and a few hastily set-up tents. A man wearing glasses was trying to light some charcoal, while another, younger man was washing out chitterlings in a big basin.

Lem parked in the lot, opposite what seemed to be the office, and asked me to find out about getting a room. A few steps beyond, there was an unlit gas pump and a 1946 or '47 Mercury in good shape. The man working at the motel told me the price of the room, but warned me they were on strike and that we'd have to make our own beds. He also told me that we'd have to go to the outskirts of Junta Grande, where there was a truckstop, to get something to eat. He was reluctant to sell us gas because of the strike, but when Lem showed him a five-dollar bill, he explained what we'd have to do to make the pump work for free. I took the opportunity to fill the tank and two ten-liter gas cans I found tossed out in back. I also raised the hood to check the oil; the last change had been made in Asunción, Paraguay.

Lem gave me the key and went to see if the telephone was working. I put the two gas cans in the trunk while the Automobile Club man stared at the car as if it were a flying saucer. He asked so many questions, I thought there might be a problem involving the police, so I told him we were coming back from Punta del Este. I don't know why I did that. I didn't have any matters pending with the police, and it didn't seem Lem was taking special precautions, but I had a vague, undefinable foreboding that impelled me to protect him.

We got to the truckstop, found a table in back, and then he asked me jokingly why I'd called him "mister."

"I don't know," I answered, "it just came to me. It could just as easily have been something else."

"Did the fortune-teller tell you anything about me?"

"That you'd bring me problems."

"That just might be the case. We can part company anytime you like."

"Not interested in the computer stuff anymore?"

"More than ever, but I wouldn't want anyone to have problems because of me. Are you still going to . . . Where was it you said you were going?"

"It doesn't matter. What kind of trouble?"

"I don't know. I never brought anyone luck."

"Are you from Brazil?"

"No. Not particularly. But better not ask me anything."

"Fine. The calculations you asked me to make are almost ready. The problem came up in the second dozen, right?"

"Seventeen and twenty-one. Did you solve it?"

"I already told you it's useless."

"You're an incurable pessimist, but I'm going to make you rich."

"Or give me problems."

"Of that you can be sure."

He took his glasses out of a leather case and asked me if I'd prefer an '82 Torrontés or an '85 Burgundy.

14 He had to settle for a Rodas, which wasn't as bad as he thought it would be, but after his coffee he ordered a French cognac. He didn't seem to realize where he was or what he was doing. The waiter asked him to repeat the brand and then asked him what it was. He gave us a strange look, perhaps because we had a few bruises from the fight and because we just didn't fit in with the place. Finally he offered us a Reserva San Juan, and Lem asked me if it was worthwhile taking a chance on it before going to sleep. I reminded him that there was a bottle of Rémy Martin in the car and suggested we have a drink back at the motel. I was struck by the way he devoured his steak, as if he'd never eaten meat before in his life.

He paid and was going to leave an excessive tip, but I pointed out that it wasn't a place frequented by the wealthy. Making a gesture of displeasure, he took back part of the change, and glanced at me to see whether what was left on the table was enough. I looked over the check and said it was. When we got back to the car, I couldn't resist the temptation any longer and asked if he was as rich as he seemed. He looked at me for a moment as if he wanted to tell me something, but ended up starting the car. We drove back in silence. When we reached the Automobile Club, he parked next to the Mercury, in which some kids were sleeping. The people from the bus were eating standing up near the fire, where the remnants of some ribs were still roasting. Lem supposed they were gypsies passing through, but what caught my attention was that he referred to the bus as a jitney.

"I'm going to need a computer," I told him as I gathered up my clothes.

He looked at the wet fields and inhaled the smell of oats.

"You take care of it; it's your business." That sounded like an order, which I didn't like.

"*My business?*" I shouted. "Do you really think you can find a computer around here?"

"Why not? Don't be such a pessimist, man. Use the car if you need it."

"You're used to having other people take care of your problems, right?"

He looked at me with an unbearable languor. The world only existed to make things more difficult for him. He took a bottle and two glasses out of the glove compartment and slammed the door after he got out.

"I'd like to speak to you alone," he said. He was standing under the glare of the motel sign.

"Alone? We've been alone for hours."

"Just long enough to have a drink," he insisted, holding up an empty glass. "Madame Nadia gave me good news."

"All right. Get the key and wait for me in the room."

He didn't even know how to do that. He said hello to the man who was still on strike and put on his eyeglasses to look over the key board. Finally he found the key and went out toward the motel without looking at me. I took the opportunity to ask the employee if I could use the telephone.

"I already told the other gentleman no. It's only for the Automobile Club."

I didn't make a scene and went out to the parking lot. The people who'd been setting up tents found some apples and pears for dessert, and one of them was tuning up a double-bass. Mercedes Sosa was singing on the Mercury's radio, but the boy had turned on his Walkman and was listening to something that must have been more exciting. He was wearing jeans and a polo shirt and had blond hair cut very short. As soon as he saw me smoking, he gestured for me to offer him a cigarette. I took out the pack, lit one up for him, and congratulated him for the car, but he didn't seem to hear me. The Walkman blocked his ears, and, nodding his head, he followed the rhythm of a band that played only for him. I raised my voice to ask him where he was going, and without taking out his earphones, he gestured for me to follow him to the car. He'd stuck the photo of a city with skyscrapers on the windshield: on the photo it said "Cleveland, Ohio." Just above that he had a decal of Mickey Mouse and another of Bariloche. On the backseat, a girl was sleeping, wrapped in a motorcycle jacket. The boy made a thumbs-up sign to tell me everything was all right and then brought his fingers together to ask me what was wrong with me.

"Bolivia," I shouted, just to say something, and he instantly nodded his approval. We smoked in silence, leaning on the hood of the Mercury, and after a while he pointed toward the people with the tents and began imitating someone playing the violin. I couldn't understand him, but I pretended I did and waved good-bye. Again he gave me the thumbs-up sign and then immersed himself once more in the guitars and drums on the Walkman. I crossed the lot, said hello to a woman putting out the fire they'd used to roast the ribs, and went to see what Lem wanted.

I found him leaning against the window, a glass in one hand and his eyes focused on the black storm clouds. He passed me the cognac and asked if I knew where we were. I said I didn't have the slightest idea and that it was all the same to me.

"Which computer do you need?" he asked, as if we were in a position to choose.

"Any computer with enough memory for me to load a mathematical program into it."

He looked at me as if I were speaking in Chinese and berated me for not having told him sooner.

"There is another solution," I said, "providing we can find a telephone."

"Are you serious?"

"I can dictate the program to a friend, but we'd have to call Italy."

"No problem!" he exclaimed, with a gesture of relief. "I'll fix it with the man in the office."

"Try," I said. "What did you want to talk to me about?"

"About you," he said, standing up to fill his glass. He brought a chair close to the veranda; he was still a mess, but the drinks were lifting his spirits. His hair was matted and he had a nice bruise above his eyebrow. That consoled me, because I didn't remember landing a single punch on his face. At that time of day, his age showed, especially in the lines under his eyes and in his voice, which was tired.

"You aren't interested in money either, right?" he asked me point-blank.

I looked at him, for the thousandth time trying to imagine a country or a planet suitable for him.

"No, I'm not interested in money, but the difference is that you have it and I don't."

"Of course, but I did nothing to earn it, let me assure you of that."

"That doesn't change things very much. What do you want to know?"

"Nothing. I hate curiosity. With your permission, I'm going to propose a gentlemen's agreement with you."

"What about?"

"I need you to hand the casino's money over to someone. My half, you understand; the other half is yours."

"Why don't you do it yourself?"

"I won't be able to."

"I've already told you the method doesn't work. You can't control luck."

"There must be a logic," he protested. "There are thirty-seven numbers and a ball, right."

"Better take it up with God."

"That's all taken care of."

"Good. To your health then."

I raised the glass and saw the reflection of a smile in his eyes. He had to prove something to someone, and money didn't matter. He was asking me to carry the proof of his victory. Suddenly he stood up and said he was going to talk to the man in charge. I watched him walk out into the twilight with his shoulders slumped and wondered why I didn't tell him he was crazy. It wouldn't have made any difference, because he was determined to play roulette with or without a program. I picked up the keys he'd left on the night table and went to the car to get my bag. The boy was back inside the Mercury, and the people with the tents were putting out the lamps. I got out my things and listened to Lem argue with the motel employee. I realized the man was wasting Lem's time and trying to get money out of him. I opened the door and, in a dry voice, asked when we were going to be able to call.

"Not even if I were drunk!" said the employee. "I'm not going to risk my job for ten dollars."

"Five," I corrected. "The gentleman said five."

The two of them stood there staring at me. I suddenly felt myself getting mad. I would have started a shouting match with them or with anyone else. I was just fed up with bouncing back and forth between them like a rubber ball.

"He showed me ten," said the man, pointing to the hand in which Lem held the money.

"Now it's five," I cut him off, pushing Lem out of the office.

"Listen, what does it matter?" Lem protested, trying to go back in.

"Exactly. Since you don't do anything to win, at least defend yourself, you fool!"

"Don't you insult me like that!"

"You're always going to lose, Mister Lem. Just as you did in Colonia Vela when you let her go, just as you did in Rio or in Alaska—"

We were standing opposite the window. I looked into his eyes, taking careful note of his hands because I thought he was going to hit me again.

"Poor jerk!" he interrupted me. "You're a shadow, nothing more than a shadow passing by. A man who goes around spying on others, picking butts up off the ground . . . Have you taken a good look in the mirror lately?"

I was so stupid that I actually did look into the window and saw myself in the trousers he'd lent me. I looked like a clown and couldn't think of anything to say. I turned away and walked toward the room knowing he was looking at me compassionately.

That night he didn't come to the room to sleep, and I imagined he'd slept in the Jaguar. I decided to finish the program and ask the kids in the Mercury to take me out of there. I checked the equations and, after making a fresh copy, got into bed. I'd barely turned off the light when the motel man knocked at my door to tell me that my friend had told him to go to hell, but that he liked me and was willing to do us the favor we'd requested.

It rained again during the night, and when I woke up, I saw a color in the sky I'd never seen before. From the window it looked like a streamer hanging over the plains. The curve wrapped around the stars, and from that same direction, dragged along by the wind, came a languid symphony. I got dressed and went out to the parking lot. For me, that hour and that light had always been the time for departure and omens. The Jaguar and the Mercury were still there, but the bus was gone and the tents with it. Beyond the Automobile Club office, a wire fence stretched into the distance, protecting a world that was alien and hostile to me.

Suddenly I remembered I'd dreamed about exactly that: I was in a suffocating labyrinth, and no matter how much I walked I was always in the same place. Something aroused me, perhaps uncertainty or my own fear, and I started running in no particular direction. I saw a man who'd climbed a telephone pole and was looking into the distance. I thought he was looking for the same thing I was, but I quickly realized he was cutting the wires, while another man on the ground stripped and rolled them up with professional skill. The copper was washed clean, and the rolls piled on the side of the road shone like the halos of saints. The two thieves paused, surprised by my silent running. In the distance, where the asphalt began to fade, I could make out the silhouettes of the musicians and the piano that looked like a gigantic coffin watched over by a demented musical society. I thought that if God did exist, he was there, mixed in with the musicians, dictating the last psalm or inaugurating the last judgment. The people from the 152 bus were there, playing a requiem that was solemn though not sad, while on the horizon there appeared a shard of reddish light. The musicians looked like ghosts who from time to time would stretch out an arm to turn a page of the score. The wind puffed out their shirts and skirts and occasionally blew the sheets off their music stands. The girl at the piano had red hair, or perhaps it was the reflection of the sunrise. One of the cellists was missing a lens from his glasses, and the double-bass player had to bend over to play his instrument, which was slowly sinking into the mud.

The thieves came over to where I was, sat down on the coils of copper, and listened with their mouths open. When the sun came up, it was as if we were all naked. The piano became blacker, and its open top made it look like a huge bird knocked down by the storm. There were twelve or fifteen musicians bidding farewell, without anger, to something they'd loved a lot and for too long. There were no other colors than those in the splendid sky, and the grays in the fields seemed to me of an overwhelming melancholy. Mozart must have been giving them his approval and they felt it, because they had smiles of jubilation on their faces. Until everything finished.

The apotheosis of the final notes vanished in a cortege of small men and women who marched off like ants getting ready for a long winter. They got together and hoisted the piano onto the bus with a rope and tied it to the bumper. When the 152 pulled out, it left a dust cloud behind that was slow to settle. For a few moments, I tried to retain that fugitive image and looked for the thieves so I could lean on something more solid than my own poor memory. Now that it was daylight, the thieves hid the rolls of wire in the grass so someone else could come by and pick them up. They paid no attention to me; one of them said hello and asked me if I were on foot. I answered that I was, that it wasn't important, and walked down the center of the road looking at the denuded poles. Later, a Harley-Davidson with a sidecar passed by and vanished into the distance. I went back slowly, and on the side of the road I found a small porcelain cup that had fallen from a pole. I remembered how when I was a kid we broke them with our slingshots, and that made me slightly sad.

Without knowing why, I put it in my pocket and walked along rubbing my fingers over it while I thought about my years in high school, when I thought I had a life ahead of me.

16   The kids in the Mercury were making breakfast, and when the boy saw me coming he gave me a friendly wave. He was still enveloped in his Walkman, so the car radio was playing exclusively for his girlfriend, who was spreading a tablecloth, unconcerned that the ground was wet. Lem was still asleep, propped against the Jaguar's windshield, desperate, badly shaven, still wearing his suit. I went into the room to fetch my bag and came back with what little I had: a handful of maté, a bar of chocolate, and the half bottle of cognac. I asked the girl if I could have a few matés with them, and she answered yes, that she'd already put the water to boil. She had intensely green eyes and an intelligent, warm way of looking that reminded me of someone else, far away. I concluded that by now she must have heard every kind of flattery, every line in the world, even though she hadn't faced the hardest thing of all yet. I handed her the Swiss chocolate, and she stared at it awhile, in shock.

"That's nothing," I told her. "Just look."

I handed her the bottle, and after she read the label, she asked me if the Jaguar were mine.

"No, it belongs to that man over there." I pointed to Lem, who had changed position and was now asleep draped over the steering wheel.

The boy, who was sitting on one of the car rugs, took a look at what I'd brought and raised his thumb, satisfied. I asked him if he'd heard any music coming from the fields, but he didn't answer me. Perhaps he was mute, but I didn't dare ask. He went to the Mercury, to which they'd attached a heater, and brought the almost boiling water. The boy handed me the maté gourd and gestured for me to make it very strong. While I put the leaves into the water, I asked him if they had permission to enter the United States. The boy took out his earphones and brought his ear close so I'd repeat the question. Then he stood up, went to the car, and came back with their passports, as if he felt obliged to show them to everyone. They were already married, and that disappointed me a bit, though I don't know why. Her name was Rita, with a Jewish or Polish last name that reminded me of Lem's. His name was Boris, he had a degree in physics, and they both had temporary visas. I congratulated him, but he shook his head as if he still had doubts about something.

"Do you know how to get to the Pan-American Highway?" Rita asked.

"I don't even know where we are right now," I said, handing her a frothy maté. "Did you ask the man from the Automobile Club?"

"He's been on strike for a week now."

Boris nodded and began to chew a cracker, waiting his turn with the maté.

"Do you know where the people with the bus were going?" I asked her.

"No, we've run into them twice already."

We went on drinking maté until Lem woke up and went to relieve himself behind the gas pump. He probably hadn't noticed we were there. Rita asked me who he was.

"A lost banker," I said, smiling.

"And you?"

"I'm just passing through," I explained, and that seemed enough for her.

Since the herb was almost gone, I steeped the last maté for her and looked at her eyes. She had a transparent, almost anguishing beauty. Lem went back to the car stretching his arms, and then he noticed we were there. He took a long drink from a bottle, straightened his tie in the car mirror and then came over to us as if he knew everyone. He shook hands with the boy, nodded to the girl, and looked at me resentfully.

"Did you finish?"

"We have to make the call."

"Whenever you like," he said, lighting a cigarette. Just then, Rita repeated something I never would have said to Lem: "So you're a lost banker?"

Lem looked at her nervously, shot me a murderous glance, and asked her where she'd gotten such an idea.

"Just a joke," she answered, probably sensing his discomfort.

"What does it matter?" said Lem, looking out at the vastness of the landscape. "Anything's possible . . . ," he added. "God throws us out here, and if we don't like the place, we start looking for another. I'm sure you're looking for your own. So, miss, I beg you to invent a more stimulating profession for me."

Rita was slightly disconcerted by his answer and repeated that it was just a joke. The music I'd heard at dawn was still echoing in my head, but now I was in good company, and that was enough for me. Rita told us about a Korean preacher they'd run into on the road. He was driving a very old Ford and would stop to redeem souls in the towns of the province. Near Lobos, someone had stabbed him in the leg. When they'd met him, he was still limping and talking to himself.

We amused ourselves telling travel stories while Lem stared at us with curiosity. Breakfast banished my fatigue. I had a vague emotion in my soul and a desire to do someone some good, so I took out the paper with the calculations on it and passed it to Lem. That brought him back to reality. He reminded me I had to call Italy and handed me his wallet so he wouldn't have to take out money in front of the others. I got up and, with a banknote in my hand, went to awaken the attendant. I mentioned that the telephone wires had been stolen, but he told me it didn't matter, that the ones who got screwed were the people in Junta Grande.

It took me half an hour to get the long-distance operator and another half hour to reach Rome. Finally I heard the voice of my friend, who asked me where I was. I tried to describe the landscape, told him I'd just heard Mozart, and when I finished my story, he told me I was lucky, that he envied me with all his heart.

17 I gave the attendant the five dollars and left the office. Lem had listened to the conversation and was waiting for me on the walkway. The numbers I'd dictated in Italian must have been dancing around in his head, and as soon as he saw me he seized the paper I had in my hand.

"But I don't understand any of this," he said, slightly disappointed, taking off his glasses.

"I'll explain it all to you right now. Wait for me in the room."

I went back to the kids to find out if there was any room for me in the car until the next service station. Boris nodded enthusiastically, pointing to the backseat. Rita asked me when I wanted to leave, because they had to fix something in the car. They had to get to the Pan-American Highway and thought I might know how to get there. I advised them to fill up, explaining what they had to do to get the gas free while I distracted the attendant.

I walked into the office and glanced at the map. There was no Junta Grande; Triunvirato and Colonia Vela were also missing. I asked the man about it, and he explained he'd been sent the wrong map, but that by now he was used to seeing it there and that it made no difference to him which map he used. In any case, he observed, no member of the Automobile Club ever came to those parts, at least since he had the job.

"Don't you even have a tow truck?"

"What for? Anyone who comes through here is already finished," he answered, settling into his chair.

"Is there a police station around here?"

"There used to be a highway patrol station, but now they're all out trying to catch rustlers. You saw the people with the bus and the roast they had. They were carrying a whole steer—didn't you notice?"

"I didn't. Listen, how can I get to the Pan-American Highway?"

"It's not easy from here. You have to go to Las Flores and cross through Cañuelas."

"How do I get to Las Flores?"

"Don't ask me for any more information—I'm on strike. Ask at the traffic circle."

I thanked him and went to get my bag. Boris was under the Mercury with a toolbox, and Rita told me that in a little while we'd be able to get back on the road. She smiled and from time to time touched her hair, which cascaded down her back.

"Do you know the United States?" she asked.

"A little. Los Angeles, San Francisco . . ."

"Ohio?" She had trouble saying it.

"No. Only from movies."

"We're going to miss this country," she said; a shadow passed over her face. I shouted to Boris to check the oil and water, and he answered me with two whistles of approval. At the other end of the patio, Lem paced back and forth outside the room with a glass in his hand, waiting for me to give him the solution to his puzzle. He'd showered and changed and was as elegant as he'd been before the fight. I asked him to go out to the car because I too wanted to drink something strong.

He sat behind the wheel and I returned his wallet and the notebook. That calmed him, and then I began to explain the results just as the computer had churned them out. His eyes glistened like those of a child listening to a fairy tale. Maybe he only needed that, and for a moment I thought everything would end there, but soon I realized it wasn't so: he started rooting around in the glove compartment, took out a yellow envelope, and before giving it to me asked if I was still willing to respect our agreement. I said I was and asked if we were running a risk of being sent to jail. Listening to myself, I felt like a rat, but Lem told me to calm down, that there was nothing illegal in breaking a casino's bank.

"Where do you want to meet?" he asked.

"I don't know; you decide."

"I need two or three days, that's all. The fortune-teller told me that after the first night I'd have a run of good luck."

"Where will you do it?"

"What difference does it make to you? I'm giving you half, right? I'm getting sick and tired of you butting into my business."

"Look, Lem, I don't know who you are or where you come from or even if we're ever going to see each other again. I'm not interested in your money. We met at one crossroads, and we'll part at another. That's it. Don't take me for a fool."

He lowered his head, opened the bottle, and poured enough in his glass to restore the morale of a battalion.

"What are you running away from?" I asked.

He looked up, emptied the glass in one swallow, and leaned his elbows on the steering wheel.

"I don't know anymore . . . I lost my way."

"That I can understand. All the signs have been torn down."

"I'm going one way, you're going another. A lady I knew preferred to stay where she was. She'd been through lots of rough times, she said. But I'm going to make my last bet. What do you say we meet on the road three days from now and have dinner together? You just keep going straight, and I'll catch up to you."

"What does 'straight' mean?"

"I mean just don't cross the wire fence."

"No danger of that."

"Signal to me."

"Agreed."

I asked him to leave me some provisions and shook his hand.

It was the first time, and it felt a little moist, but perhaps that was because he'd just showered—and even shaved and combed his hair. I opened the door, and then I remembered the little cup I'd picked up on the road. I handed it to him through the window, twirling it with my fingers.

"Take it, just for luck. Luck you can always use."

"This time it won't get away from me," he said, starting the engine.

He hesitated a moment before deciding which way to go, finally heading toward the traffic circle where we'd been the night before. I waved to him and walked out to the road to watch him drive off. When I got back to the room, I opened the envelope he'd left me, but all I found inside was an old photo. It was a boy nine or ten years old, wearing a smock, with eyes identical to Lem's and with his hair falling over his forehead. He was alone on an unrecognizable sidewalk, carrying a school satchel. Someone had asked him to smile. In one hand, he held a spinning top that had split right down the center.

18 Before nightfall, I went out to walk along the wire fence. Because of the rain, the wild daisies had reappeared, clumped together in the grass on the side of the road. I went quite far because I thought the kids in the Mercury wanted to be alone. I stopped opposite the gate where I'd listened to the requiem and sat on the bridge to rest awhile.

Just a thin line of sun remained on the horizon when I looked at my watch and realized it had stopped. The crystal was broken and moisture clouded its entire face. That made me sad because it was the only souvenir I had left of my father. I took it off and put it in my pocket, thinking that perhaps I could get it fixed when I got someplace. I was getting depressed and had begun to rummage around in the things that pained me most, when I heard a noise like pots and pans bouncing on the ground.

I turned around and discovered a man dragging an enormous valise while he picked something up in the weeds. He wore a rubber hose wrapped around his waist, a pin with Perón's face on it, and the closer he got the more the air smelled of cheap perfume. His entire being was a mistake, and there, out in the open country, it was obvious at first sight. He didn't see me and must have thought he was alone on the pampa because he let the noise of his stomach gas escape and then went to urinate on the asphalt. His legs swung like seesaws and his long arms stood out from his cuffs. His suit was roomy and missing almost all its buttons. His trousers were so baggy in the knees they could never be pressed. He looked at both sides of the road and began to talk, as if to keep himself company.

He seemed to be broadcasting a soccer match or something while he put the things that had fallen out of his suitcase back in order. I wanted to light a cigarette, but I didn't want him to see me and find myself in an uncomfortable situation. I also couldn't move from where I was without crossing his path, so I was forced to remain still for a long time. Finally, when the man was some distance away, I stood up and began to walk along the wire fence. Suddenly I tripped over something and slipped down to the bottom of the ditch. That made quite a noise, and when I got up I heard the man running toward me. I lit a cigarette, took a few puffs, and looked for a clearing where I could climb back up to the road. I couldn't see where I was walking, but I could make out the rolls of copper wire hidden by the thieves with the motorcycle. I wanted to get away, but now it was too late. Totally out of breath, the big man looked down from the shoulder of the road, and asked me if I could tell him how to get to the outskirts of Triunvirato.

"My partner was supposed to meet me at eight," he said, "but something must have happened to him."

I climbed up, slipping and hanging on to bushes, until finally he held out his hand and pulled me out with one tug. He had a thick mustache, and his eyes were as small as chickpeas.

"I'm on foot," I told him. "Not because I like to be."

"But someone's going to pick you up," he insisted. "They won't leave you stranded out here with the merchandise."

It didn't seem worthwhile explaining anything. We were there, and no matter what he thought, it was all the same.

"I don't know what time it is," I answered. "My watch broke."

He looked at his and told me it was ten to nine.

"Now that's a good business to be in." He pointed to the telephone poles without wires. "I wanted to go and cut wire in Bahía Blanca, but to do that you need a pickup."

"Some people make do with a motorcycle," I said.

"Sure, but either way you've got to have capital." The brilliantine he used was solid enough to keep his hair plastered down. "We've got to suffer the worst things, pal. If they let us private citizens work, we'll get ahead. Look at the wealth we have . . ."

With one arm he encompassed the immense countryside as if it all belonged to him. Then he rested his arm on the hose. He must have had the strength of a truck to drag all that around.

"Been around here for a long time?" I asked.

"Three or four months. I was hitchhiking to Mendoza, but since nobody ever came by, I ended up staying. . . . Now I try to pick up what I can in this part of the country."

"That must be uncomfortable," I said, pointing to the hose.

"Sure is. They say that now they make one that weighs less than a handkerchief. In Japan, everybody washes with one of these."

He went over to the valise and began to pull at the lock. But it was no use. It was stuck, and no matter how hard he kicked it, he got nowhere.

"You just open up and you've got an extendable shower, see? The hose part connects to any faucet or to the well pump."

"I see. What do you use it for?"

"I go from ranch to ranch washing sharecroppers. My wife died a little while back, and I had to leave my kid in Berazátegui."

"Rough . . ."

"He's with his grandfather. I have to send some money, but for now . . ."

"I'm staying in the Automobile Club," I told him. "If your partner doesn't show up, come over and have a beer."

"At the motel? Shit, that's the kind of work I like! I always say you've got to change with the times, that if the State would leave us alone, everything would fix itself in a year. And you, how much wire do you cut in a day?"

"I don't know, I don't take care of . . ."

Just then he grabbed my arm and pointed up the road. Two small lights, like lanterns, were approaching in jumps.

"A car!" he shouted, and ran to cover up his valise. "Hide—you never know if they're going to stop!"

I walked away, taking the opportunity to cross to the opposite shoulder. The big man went out onto the roadway, waving as the lights came closer. I walked a little further, and when I heard the sound of the motor, I turned around to see what was happening. The Citroën hit the pavement, swerved aside, and kept on going as if it had seen nothing. I recognized that arrogance, which is why I would have preferred that Nadia stop and pick the man up.

19 Walking away, I could hear the big man first curse a blue streak and then start broadcasting a brand-new game. It must have helped him kill time while he waited for his partner to pick him up. I went back to the motel to see if the kids were ready to get going, but they too had gone

out for a walk. The attendant was eating charcoal-broiled beef and salad; maybe he was preparing himself for when the gas ran out, or maybe he just decided to sit back and wait for something to happen. He must have made a serious mistake for the company to have exiled him to that place. Whenever I saw the telephone, I was tempted to call my daughter, but I wasn't sure she'd want to hear from me after such a long time. I was tired of putting up with myself, just as Nadia had said, but I didn't have enough courage either to go on or to go back. Perhaps Coluccini was right when he told me never to hit the brakes, and now I felt a certain pleasure in just drifting along, like a fallen leaf.

I took a chair out of the room and sat in the shade with a beer and a can of sardines. Lem had paid for several nights. If I ever found him again, he'd go right on paying, because for some strange reason he had to do it. I didn't believe a word he told me about the casino, but I thought he must have had his reasons for telling me that story instead of a different one.

It must have been midnight when I heard a motorbike—it was coming down the road with its lights off. The kids still hadn't come back, so I stretched out in bed to read one of the novels Lem had left me. Later, when the attendant turned out the light, a woman ran across the yard shouting; then she started pounding on his door with both hands, as if there were some emergency. The man pretended not to hear, and her demands became even more insistent. The woman insulted him, and when that got no response, she threw stones at the office. For a while, I listened to her monotonous sobbing, which was more from spite than rage. Finally a window shattered, and she ran back across the yard calling him a cowardly son of a bitch, accusing him of having ruined her life and that of someone named Julia. The place was covered with rocks, so the man played it safe and kept out of sight.

I fell asleep and woke up several times, but the combination of the heat and the argument cured my sleepiness. I read for a while, unable to concentrate, afraid the woman would come back. I opened the window to cool off the room, and a locust flew in, as dry and brown as the one I'd seen on Lem's bed. It landed on the lamp, near the crucifix, and stayed there, projecting an enormous, deformed shadow over the page I was reading. At first, I paid it no attention, but after a bit, when I tried to find my place, it jumped and landed right on my face. I was scared out of my wits, and when I slapped it off, it flew out the same way it had come in. I wanted to go back to the book, but I had something in my eye, some dirt that bothered me when I winked.

I got up to look at myself in the mirror, but the light was weak, and I saw nothing. I tried to brush the dirt out of my eye with my handkerchief, but that was useless because my hand was shaking badly. I got back into bed and contemplated the insects flying around the lamp. An hour or more must have gone by when I heard someone else out in the yard. Finally, there was a knock at my door, and my heart pounded, as if I were expecting a visit from a pair of big green eyes. I jumped out of bed and opened the door without realizing I was almost naked.

"Sorry, comrade, but my partner stood me up."

The big man had left his suitcase on the ground next to him and was wiping his forehead with a handkerchief. He'd stuck some gold letters on the valise that read: BARRANTE INSTANT SHOWERS. He must have been proud of his cleverness because he'd also sewn the same words onto the sleeves stitched to his jacket. With the hose wrapped around him up to his neck, he looked like a roll of dried beef. He must have noticed the disappointment on my face, because he gestured as if to pick up the valise and leave. On his forearm he wore a wide, shiny mourning band which I hadn't seen earlier. I told him to come have a beer with me and looked out toward the motel's entranceway. I wished I could have found something else, but all I saw were the silvery reflections of the Mercury.

20 "It looks like I've come at a bad time," Barrante said, standing stock-still in the middle of the room. Once again, I had the sensation that everything about him was an error. In his small eyes, there was naïveté but also the cunning of someone who's on his own and ready for anything.

"Don't worry. I couldn't sleep anyway."

"And with all that noise they were making right outside your door here."

"Not my door, it was for the guy from the Automobile Club."

"All the same, you look down in the dumps, man. I mean, if you don't mind my saying so."

"Make yourself at home."

I pointed to a chair and got two cans of beer out of my bag.

"You can't imagine how long it's been since I had a beer."

"A shame it isn't cold," I said. "Got the time?"

He looked at a plastic watch he had hanging around his neck on a little chain, with the image of Saint Caetano.

"Twenty after two. I was waiting for half an hour on the other side of the road, but I couldn't get up the courage to come over. I don't like getting in the way, understand?"

He loosened up the hose and asked permission to sit on the bed. The hose was so tight it caused his face to swell with blood, turning his nose and cheeks red.

"Don't you want to take all that off?"

"Well, it's that I don't know where I'm going to sleep tonight," he said, looking at the pillow.

"If your snoring's not too loud, you can stay here. I don't think the man from the office will poke his nose in."

"You're not kidding?" He looked at me for a moment, suspended between happiness and surprise. "Don't you want to be alone, buddy?"

"It's all the same to me."

"I don't know. . . . It looked to me like when I came in you were . . . I don't know, you don't have to be a woman to cry, right? It happens to me from time to time."

He made me smile. His nights must not have been any easier than mine.

"Are you saying that because you saw tears? It's that I've got some dirt in my eye."

"Really?" He was still studying me. "Want me to take a look?"

"I'd appreciate it."

He slipped the hose over his head as if it were a sweater. He seemed nervous as he set the roll down on the floor, under the wash basin.

"Let's see now. Rest your head on the pillow."

I let him go on because my eye was burning as if a hot coal were embedded in it. He turned on the lamp and brought it closer while he raised my eyelids with two pudgy and filthy fingers. His breath was bitter, and his teeth were covered with yellow plaque. Everything he had on was falling apart, and the Perón button was just about to fall off his lapel.

"Now I see it," he said. "I'm good at this sort of thing, just relax."

I wanted to ask him what brand of brilliantine he used but didn't want to interrupt his work. He was trying his best, even though he'd covered many, many miles on foot, and his feet must have been a mess. He dragged the valise to the foot of the bed and opened it, using his foot as a crowbar. The shower head popped up next to my face, thrust upward by a system of interlocking pipes controlled by a spring mechanism. Then he attached the hose to the faucet in the sink and looked me in the eye again.

"I've got it, pal," he said, and turned on the water without telling me.

Several of the holes in the shower head were blocked and others shot the water out every which way, so in a minute or so we'd soaked the entire room. I kept my eye open as long as I could while he washed it out, and, to tell the truth, it relieved me instantly. As he turned off the faucet, he seemed as proud as a fireman who's done his duty.

"What do you think of that?" He beamed, leaning against the door frame.

"Outstanding," I confessed.

"I can even get out splinters with this thing," he said. "As for bugs, they don't stand a chance. If I add a little insecticide, there isn't a flea in the world that can stand up to me. Things of that sort, it goes without saying, are not in the manual they give you."

"Experience is the best teacher," I said, to please him.

"Experience and brains, buddy." He tapped his forehead with a finger. "If I only had money!"

"Have a seat."

"I earned my beer, right?" He took a swallow and licked the drops that had eluded him by slipping over the edge of the can. "I can't figure out what happened to my partner. It isn't like him not to show up."

"Maybe the car broke down."

"Maybe. He's got an old heap. Tell me, if you don't mind, how many of you are there?"

"How many of who?"

"How many of you are in the wire business. You wouldn't need another man, would you?"

"I don't have anything to do with it. I just happened to be passing by."

"Listen now, I don't want you to think I'm a cop."

"No, I'm telling you the truth. The guys doing the wire were kids who had a motorbike."

"What a business that is! I was going to get started in it near Bahía Blanca."

"So you told me. But you need a pickup."

"A little van, anything that could carry a load. . . . Look, this week, I think I've eaten—really eaten—just twice. On Thursday in Triunvirato and the day before yesterday only because some people going around playing music offered me food."

"I can offer you a can of sardines. I think I have mackerel too."

"Sardines are enough for me. So you're not in the business?"

"No, I was just passing by."

He looked disappointed. Without saying a word, he took off his shoes, whose soles were quite perforated, and stretched his legs out on top of the bed. Only the tops of his socks were left, and his feet were so swollen they looked like pumpkins.

"The police must be around here," he said. "That's why my partner didn't show up."

I handed him another beer, and he ate the sardines in one mouthful. Paying no attention to me, he lay down and pounded the mattress with his hands.

"I'm fed up with washing field hands," he whispered, as if to himself.

"You're from Buenos Aires, right?"

He nodded his head, with a touch of pride.

"From Floresta," he said. "Three blocks from the All Boys soccer field."

"You couldn't find any other work?"

"What?" he asked, as if he'd suddenly awakened. "Other work . . . If I had money I'd go with my partner, but I don't want to get too far away from my kid. Every once in a while I have to send him something, right?"

"Where's your partner going?"

"I don't know. A place where there's free enterprise."

"I thought you had faith in the country," I said, pointing to his pin.

"I do have faith, but it's rough to hit bottom. I don't know, if I had ten showers instead of one, I could set up a little business. You saw me work, right? I'm a serious person. I'd hire ten Paraguayans, and in a year I'd be doing fine."

"Aren't you making it seem too easy?"

"No. Just look at the priest my partner drives around: he says Mass for the field hands, he marries them, he baptizes them, he reads them the Bible, whatever. . . . He can't handle all the work. He took on two employees to cover the whole zone and makes a mountain of money."

"A real priest?"

"Absolutely. A priest who took off on his own and now has his own business. Look: he's got his name down for a plan to buy a Renault Twelve."

"They'll throw him in jail."

"Never, he wears a cassock and everything. The helpers are phonies, but that's their worry—he always tells them that."

"Do they say Mass too?"

"I don't know. I think they chase the devil off the farms and remove hexes from women, or something like that. The priest teaches them. He offered me a job, but I'd have to have a cassock. And it seems they're really expensive."

"What do you say we sleep for a while."

"You're the boss."

He didn't say another word. He stretched out on the bed with his face to the wall and fell asleep just like that. It took me a little longer. I locked the door, turned out the lights, and thought that I'd met more people in the past few days than I had in all the years I lived in Europe.

21 Boris woke me up and invited me to lunch. He rapped on the window and brought his hand to his mouth to show they had something delicious. Barrante had gone off early and left a piece of cardboard on the night table inscribed with his slogan and a word of thanks. I washed up and

shaved, happy for having slept well and because my eye had stopped bothering me.

The kids found charcoal near the pump, and Boris was tending the grill where a big armadillo, skin and all, was roasting. Rita shook my hand as if I were a stranger and told me that the Automobile Club attendant was barricaded in his office with a loaded shotgun and enough food for several days, but that it was possible to negotiate with him.

"There are two women who throw stones at him," she said. "Julia is the nicer of the two."

"Is it about the strike?"

"No." She smiled as if I couldn't possibly understand. "It's about the sorrows of love."

"That's what it sounded like to me last night," I said.

She stood still for a moment in silence, staring at the coals.

"If you want to talk to him, wave a white handkerchief as you approach. He doesn't trust anyone."

"I wouldn't dream of it. Did you two go hunting?"

"I wouldn't exactly call it hunting," she said, pointing to the armadillo. "Once they come out of their holes, it's easy to grab them."

Boris piled up the coals and then pointed to the fields on the other side of the highway. He joined the fingers of both hands and traced a line on the horizon to tell me there were lots of armadillos in the wheat fields.

"Did you fill up the tank?"

Boris nodded, but grimaced to warn me something was wrong with the car.

"The transmission's broken," Rita said, "but it may be possible to fix it."

"You can't get it into high?" I ventured.

"Yes, I think that's it. Do you know anything about mechanical things?"

"No, it was just a guess. Can Boris hear us?"

The boy looked up and gestured to indicate I could speak

freely. I smiled at him, disappointed, and didn't know what to say. What disturbed me most about Rita were her eyes, which were of a green different from any other green eyes I'd ever seen. And around us almost everything else was green. Perhaps she was nothing more than a pretty girl I was idealizing because I felt incapable of seducing her. Suddenly I heard myself say out loud, without really wanting to: "I'm just passing through."

The two of them looked at me at the same time and then exchanged an uncomfortable glance. I remembered Barrante, who broadcast soccer matches, and changed the subject. I asked them if they'd seen the man with the valise leave.

"He cut right through the middle of the open country," said Rita, "that way."

I looked toward where her finger was pointing, on the other side of the wire fence, but there was nothing but drab, desolate immensity. Any one of the unmoving points I could see on the horizon could be Barrante. Boris mimicked him to show that the valise seemed very heavy. Then he tasted a piece of meat and informed us it was ready. Rita brought some hard crackers, lamenting there was nothing to drink. I remembered I had a few beers left and got up to get them. As I was crossing the parking lot in front of the motel, the attendant peered out from behind the bathroom curtain and ordered me to identify myself. I shouted out who I was, and when he recognized my voice, he told me I could go on. From the window of my room, I saw his double-barreled shotgun moving back and forth like a pair of binoculars on the watch. I came back with the beers without stopping to identify myself, and when he demanded I tell him again who I was, I told him to go screw himself. Then I asked if he could sell me something cool. The shotgun stopped moving, and he hesitated awhile before reacting.

"Identify yourself first!"

I repeated my name, and he asked me if I had anyone hidden in my room. I opened the door to show him, and he told me to leave the money on the office desk. I approached holding a handkerchief in my hand, as Rita had instructed me, and left what I thought was enough. A short time later, two cartons of wine flew through the curtain, and Boris went to pick them up with his hands over his head, as if he were in a western movie.

"At least he's not crazy," observed Rita. And when I gave her a disconcerted look, she smiled at me.

We had a sumptuous meal with plain but well-chilled wine, and we talked about the trip. Boris had dozens of photos of Cleveland he'd cut out of foreign magazines, and when we'd finished eating, he told us a long story of which I understood only a few gestures. He was nice, especially when he'd had a few drinks, and Rita respected him enough not to translate anything for me. He didn't use standard sign language but one he'd invented himself, which was neither funny nor vulgar. Perhaps he'd created it for Rita, and if that was the case, it was obviously worthwhile. I was convinced he could speak, but it didn't matter to me why he didn't. I understood he was going to fix the gear box in the afternoon, and that the next day we'd search for the Pan-American Highway. I said it was fine with me and that I was at his disposal.

Rita put away the wine and told Boris she wanted to sleep during siesta. I took that as an invitation to leave and went to my room to read awhile. From there, I could see the shotgun keeping guard over the countryside, and the Mercury, which had paper curtains hung up inside it. I spent a few hours immersed in a book and then sat for a minute staring at the wall. Then I heard some moans coming from the Mercury. They were meant for me, but the attendant became frightened and stuck his head out through the broken window. He was moving the shotgun around as if looking for a target, so to avoid trouble I crouched down and closed my curtain. I sat on the floor and began, unwillingly, to masturbate, thinking that my destiny was Nadia and the Citroën going around in circles, Lem and his casino mania, and Barrante with his dreams of free enterprise. To concentrate, I had to imagine Rita, and that was what humiliated me most, because she was still in the Mercury and knew what I was doing.

22 At sundown, I took a walk so I wouldn't have to see the kids. I went to the traffic circle and then to the restaurant where I'd had dinner with Lem. I ordered hot empanadas and asked some truckers what I had to do to reach the Pan-American Highway. They were eating noodles and stew, and when they saw me come over to their table, they looked at me as if I were a lunatic. One of them gave me the same directions the Automobile Club attendant had given me, but added that the road to Las Flores was being repaired, so I'd be better off going the long way, around Colonia Vela. They didn't pay much attention to me, and as soon as the empanadas were ready I took them outside to eat in the shade of a tree.

When I got back to the motel, I saw that the curtains were still up in the Mercury, and as I passed I heard Rita complaining in a low voice. I went toward my room, clearing my throat as loudly as I could so the attendant wouldn't confuse me with someone else, but he still ordered me to stop. I took out my handkerchief, reminded him who I was, and he told me to go through. I wasn't used to long walks, and my varicose veins were quite swollen. I opened the window, stretched out in bed with the light out, and lit a cigarette.

The stone-throwing began a few minutes later, this time without the haranguing and crying. The noise of clods smashing against the walls was disturbing; it was a more methodical attack than that of the previous night, softer and more oppressive. The woman ran around the house, and from time to time passed by my window, breathing heavily. The attendant called her "my Julia" and begged her to go back to Corrientes and let him live in peace. All hell broke loose when he mentioned the other woman, whose name was Ana; that aroused some bad memory the three of them must have been sharing for a long time. Julia answered that she would track him to the end of the world, and that's when I heard the sound of the shotgun open and close as the attendant loaded it. It was a dry *click-clack* that hit me right in the pit of my stomach. In the darkness, Julia flattened herself against my door, and without speaking too loudly, I asked her to come inside.

She didn't even answer me: I saw her slip past the window and supposed she was going to get more stones. The attendant lost sight of her and began to call her, using stupid flattery, as if they were at a dance. He talked to her awhile in Guaraní, trying to caress her through her ears, to arouse her compassion a bit, but as he went into his monologue, he was overcome by a pasty sort of melancholy, which was boring. When I turned on the lamp to undress, I heard the bang of one stone and then another. The attendant began to howl like a hurt dog, all the while beating his shotgun against the wall. It wasn't a wail of pain but the whine of a cornered animal about to attack.

I decided that was the last night I'd spend there and looked for a pen so I could leave a message for Lem. I'd just begun to write when I thought I heard the confused description of a soccer match. I leapt to my feet and turned out the light so Barrante wouldn't see I was there; then things happened very quickly. The attendant's window wasn't visible from the road, and even though he shouted for Barrante to identify himself, Barrante just walked straight toward my room, carrying his enormous valise, running one hand over his brilliantined hair.

Just then, Julia ran out, and I heard the shotgun blast, which made a long, lazy echo. Barrante put the valise on the ground, looked at me as if to excuse himself, and took out his handkerchief to mop his forehead. He still didn't understand what was happening to him: the handkerchief slipped out of his hand, and when he tried to catch it, he lost his balance. I never saw anyone fall so slowly. The hose wound around his waist kept him standing straight, so he had time to look around and to tell me his partner still hadn't turned up. I was about to tell him not to worry, but he shuddered and began to collapse, slightly embarrassed by the scene he was creating.

Rita and Boris ran over but stopped at a distance, thinking there might be more gunfire. The attendant began to shout that he was sorry, but we were all looking at Barrante, who bent his knees like a tired horse and fell over his valise with the same smile he must have worn when he appeared on the local farms. I lifted his head, and he asked me what had happened, calling me buddy, as he had before. I loosened the hose so he could breathe better and lit him a cigarette. It was then I discovered that behind his ear he had two holes, as small as the ones in the shower head. "Just when I'd stopped smoking," he said. "Because of how expensive cigarettes have gotten . . ."

Then he stared at the sky disinterestedly. I imagined he was figuring ways to get enough money together to set up his business, or perhaps he was remembering the boy he'd left in Berazategui. "I'll put you in my bed, okay?"

"Don't bother. It's so hot . . ."

He puffed on the cigarette without taking it out of his mouth, and the ash fell on his lapel. His brilliantine had withstood the violent jolt, and he still gave off the smell of cheap perfume, but he'd lost his Perón button. He looked at the shower and asked me to store it in my room because he had to get to work very early. I told him I would and went to the office to get help.

"Which highway is it?" the telephone operator asked.

"I don't know, an Automobile Club, near Junta Grande."

"Where's that?"

"There's a traffic circle next to it," I said. "I came here from Triunvirato."

"I don't know the area. Are you sure that's the name of the place?"

I asked her to look in the telephone book or call a hospital and then went outside again. Boris took off his jacket and spread it over Barrante's face. Rita told me the attendant had escaped through the back door, taking the shotgun with him. "He was crying a lot," she added sorrowfully.

I asked Boris to help me carry the body into the office, but he made me understand that it would be better if the police found him in the exact spot where he'd fallen. "Who knows if they'll think we killed him," added Rita, and although she only stepped back a few yards, I felt she was leaving me forever. I picked up the jacket, tossed it to Boris, and told both of them to go to bed. As soon as I was alone, I got out a chair and sat down to smoke alongside Barrante. From where I was, I could see his Perón button lying on the ground. A thin stream of water was running out of the hose, and I wondered if knowing he was dead mattered to anyone, if they'd cry for him over in Berazategui, even if only for a moment.

I was sure no ambulance, police, or anyone else would ever come, but all the same I didn't feel like sleeping. Two noisy horseflies were buzzing around, but soon they began flying in circles around the lamp in my room. I drank the last beer and then the wine left over from midday. It was a peaceful night, and the kids fell asleep as if nothing had happened. Coming back, I picked up the button and put it into one of his pockets. Barrante's brilliantine had given out and his face was by now undeniably that of a dead man.

I was just beginning to nod off in the chair when I heard the telephone in the office ringing. I thought someone had finally found us and ran to answer, even though I didn't like the idea of anyone crossing our path. I picked up the phone, and when I heard Lem's voice I felt less alone. He was calling to tell me he was beginning to win and that he wanted to confirm that our agreement was still holding. I said it was, although I no longer remembered exactly what the agreement was.

"I'll pick you up on the road, then."

"Relax."

"Don't get angry with me now."

"But you just told me you were winning—"

"No matter what happens, I've already won. Understand?"

"I think so," I said, but I was drunk and didn't understand a thing.

23 The Mercury pulled out during the night with its headlights turned off. The kids deliberated a long time, because I heard Rita talking in a low voice and in different tones. Maybe they reached the conclusion that they were getting into a mess, so they left without telling me. The alcohol affected me badly; for a moment I thought everything had been a dream, but when I stood up I saw that Barrante was still there, stiffer and more forsaken than ever. Dawn gave the fields a milky look—it was the time of day that made me most nervous. I got out a blanket for Barrante and made him a rather long speech about the inconveniences of free-market economies. When I finished, I vomited and went to sleep in the office armchair.

I must have slept for two days straight, because when I was awakened, it was afternoon and a light drizzle was beginning to fall. I didn't hear them come, but when I opened my eyes I found a priest with a toothpick in his mouth scrutinizing me through the window. I stumbled to my feet and saw him take off his cassock and go into the repair shop bathroom. I looked at my reflection in the glass covering the map and saw someone who looked like a boxer going down for the count. I stuck my head into the kitchen sink and from there heard someone kicking the gas pump. For a while I didn't know who I was or where I was, but little by little I began to figure things out. I took a Coke out of the refrigerator and drank it down in one gulp. As soon as I stepped out onto the patio, I recognized the totally patched-up Gordini with the valises on its roof, and immediately heard the voice of Coluccini shouting *"L'avventura è finita!"* as he went on kicking the pump.

"Fill it up, *ragazzo*," he said and took out the sheaf of bills he had ready in his pocket. I stood there staring at him, one shoulder resting against the pump, while the priest came out of the lavatory buttoning his fly.

"Don't tell me there's no more gas," the fat man protested impatiently.

"If I were you, I'd buy it in Bolivia," I said, and that surprised him a bit. He put on his glasses and dedicated a moment of attention to me, but it wasn't easy to catch him off-guard. "Good idea. I'm looking for the way out of here," he answered with a sigh, changing his glasses while he spoke to the priest, who was opening the hood. "I've seen this gentleman somewhere before."

Since he couldn't impress me, he forgot to speak Italian. The priest was a big, muscular man who was looking around to see if he could find something he could take without paying.

"Isn't there any gas?" he asked in a bullying tone, a not-exactly-friendly expression on his face.

"Well, since you ask, yes, there is gas," I said, and I began to remember the story Barrante had told me.

"Then fill it up. It's going to rain," he said.

"The gentleman helped me leave Ranchos," the fat man interjected. "So now you work for the Automobile Club?"

"It wasn't Ranchos," I said. "By the way, you wouldn't have a friend you were supposed to pick up, would you?"

"Yessir, that's where we're going. What happened was that I had some trouble with an axle, and the Father here was held up with a sick man."

"No need to hurry now." I pointed to the shape stretched out on the patio. The blanket was getting soaked and taking on the shape of a sprawled-out body. The fat man shot me a nervous look and kissed the medal he wore around his neck.

"Don't tell me there's been a tragedy!" he shouted, grasping his head in his hands.

"You'll have to inform his family."

"Not me, I barely knew him. It's the guy with the shower," he said to the priest.

"He told me he was your partner."

"Partner . . . I'd just pick him up, that's all. He owed me for three trips."

"He had a high opinion of you."

"I told him to watch out where he stuck his nose," said the priest, spitting out the toothpick. "The countryside's overrun with thugs."

"Someone's going to have to bring him to a cemetery," I said.

"How did it happen?" Coluccini asked. "Women, for sure."

"There was one, but it was all a mistake."

"Did you call the police?" Now the priest became nervous.

"No, no one's going to come."

"*Porca miseria,* now we're really screwed," grumbled the fat man. "Go on, Salinas, give him the extradition."

"Extreme unction," corrected the priest. "That's not what he's supposed to get. Where's he going to be buried?"

"Right here, wherever our friend says. I'm too old to shovel."

"Near the fence," I suggested.

The fat man went with me to get the tools, and I began to dig a grave. On the roof of the motel, several carancho buzzards kept watch, and even though I threw rocks at them, they didn't move a muscle. Coluccini put on a hat and brought me a couple of matés while the priest washed up in the service station water tank.

"I was running low on funds," he told me, "so I had to join up with these boys to work in this area for a while. I drive them to farms and pick them up afterward. They pay me, not much, but soon I'll be able to get going again, God willing. And you, did you strike oil?"

"Not exactly. I've got a partner who's going to break the bank in a casino."

"Bunk!"

"Do you think there could actually be a casino somewhere near here?"

"Could be. Salinas went to do an exorcism at a ranch where

there was a Formula I race track and a whorehouse with French whores."

"Is Salinas a real priest?"

"I don't know; look, it's none of my business. He sure can handle the Latin all right."

While the fat man brewed another maté, I took a look at Salinas, who was drying off with a bath towel next to the Gordini. He'd left his cassock hanging from the gas pump and was whistling the tune "Honeysuckle." He looked to be about thirty-five, but had very little hair left and so seemed older. He paid no attention to us: he opened a briefcase in which he carried everything and was primping as if he were getting ready to bless a cathedral. My feet got muddy the more the rain poured into the hole, and suddenly I was afraid I would die there. It was an undefinable terror that passed as soon as Coluccini came over with the maté and talked about something I didn't understand. I realized I was shaking, and to forget it I told him to help me carry Barrante's body over. The priest pretended not to hear, but the fat man insisted on the extradition thing and succeeded in getting him mad.

"That's for when someone's dying," Salinas told him. "There's nothing to do now. He's already with God."

"An Our Father wouldn't hurt him," said Coluccini, handing him the cassock. Salinas got dressed, took out a Bible, or something that looked like a Bible, and took his place on one side of the grave. He didn't look very enthusiastic, but he made the sign of the cross and cursed me for not closing the dead man's eyes. I admitted he was right and asked Coluccini to hold him up under his arms so I could unwind the hose. The two of us were going around in circles, slipping on the gravel, while Salinas prayed in a grandiloquent voice, making the sign of the cross in the storm. Without the hose, Barrante turned out to be as skinny as a strand of spaghetti, and it was then I realized he wasn't joking when he said he only ate from time to time. In the struggle, he lost what was left of his shirt, and the zipper on his fly as well. Coluccini bent over to go through his pockets, and from that position he spoke to the priest.

"Look, Father, I don't want to offend you, but the dearly departed here owed me for a couple of trips, and if you'll give me permission, I think he'd be better off meeting God with all his debts paid, or am I wrong?"

"If there are no heirs . . . ," said Salinas.

The fat man found a few loose pesos, the Perón button, a wallet with his identification papers, and some family photos. He put all of it in his jacket pocket and then signaled that we should dump him into the hole. The priest read a few verses that had nothing to do with the ceremony and pushed in a little dirt with his shoe. Coluccini tossed in the first shovelful, but he was so upset that I asked him to let me take care of it.

"No sir," he answered. "He was my partner, and a partner, even if he's a thirty percent partner, has a call on our friendship."

He took off his jacket and took a long time to seal the grave. His chest was rising and falling rapidly, and he even seemed to be moved. Long before we finished, the priest had left us to get out of the rain.

"Poor guy," said Coluccini. "It's always the ones at the bottom who get it first."

24   At dinner time, Salinas drove off in the Gordini, promising to bring us something to eat. Coluccini came to my room, unfolded a map of the province of Buenos Aires on the bed, and, after looking it over, put his finger on the border of the province of Río Negro.

"In my opinion, we're right around here."

"What makes you think so?"

"Well, you were going south, right?"

"So what?"

"This is the south." He tapped the map with his finger.

"I changed direction a couple of times."

"What? Weren't you searching for oil?"

"I was thinking of going to Neuquén. The part about the oil was something you made up."

"That's true, I get mixed up because of Barrante. He was making his way to Mendoza. Listen, if you want to work with the shower, just go right ahead. I think he was finished paying it off."

"Thanks. Which way are you going?"

"For now, whichever way the priest's going, but in a week, Zárate, I'm taking off on my own. Doesn't your partner need to be picked up? There are always mobsters outside casinos."

"Zárate's in Australia."

"Let me call you by his name. No offense: Zárate's an extraordinary man."

"You told me he ran away with your wife and kids."

"What's wrong with that? I didn't say he'd run off, I said he left."

"In that case, call me any name you please."

"Your partner, does he need to be picked up?"

"He's got a car."

"Ah, mobility's the key thing nowadays! If I could only get this thing into fourth gear, I'd be in La Paz by now."

"You've got business there?"

"I've got special videos. Triple X-rated, you know what I mean. There's a market for it in the jungle."

"It must be a dangerous place."

"It isn't. They've already entered the twenty-first century. There's no comparison with us: we're in the asshole of the world."

"Barrante was an optimist."

"Now that you mention his name . . . I pocketed some money that doesn't belong to me. Look . . ."

He dug through his pocket and put everything that belonged to the big guy on the table. The wallet, the Perón button, and a few wrinkled bills. Then I remembered that we'd buried him with his watch on.

"Look, he owed me a hundred thousand australes, and there are about three hundred thousand here. I don't know if he owed you anything."

"No, I barely knew him."

"Why don't you send the money to his family, what do you say? You must know how to write a letter."

"And where do I find a post office to mail it?"

"I don't know. Maybe you could give it to a truck driver who goes to Buenos Aires."

"If you want me to . . ."

"I mean, just so they don't go on waiting for him."

"Would you do it for me?"

"You're not my partner."

"But you gave me Zárate's name, didn't you?"

"That's true. Listen, don't turn into a bad-luck charm on me! You're going to find oil, and I'm going to get to Bolivia."

"Fine. What do I do if I find oil?"

"Sell it right away. Don't get involved in messes like that. A cousin of mine found a fortune in the Córdoba mountains and almost ruined himself."

"What kind of fortune?"

"A money bag from a bank. Ten billion incredibly old pesos, but when he tried to exchange them, he found out they were worthless. And on top of that, he was almost thrown in jail."

"Now that really is bad luck."

"Bad luck! A country where finding a fortune is a waste of time isn't a serious country, Zárate. I know what I'm talking about. I lost the circus in less than one year; I had to sell the lion . . ."

"Don't work yourself up now, you'll just get bitter."

"A preacher from La Boca in Buenos Aires bought the tent, what do you think of that?"

"Maybe you hadn't brought the show up to date . . ."

"Think so? Where do you think I got the videos? The only things I managed to salvage."

"Things are no better in Bolivia, I'm sorry to tell you."

"That's just one rung on the ladder, Zárate, I'm going much further."

"And what about this priest, where's he going?"

"Salinas is getting rich. You can't imagine the success he has with his sermons. . . . That story about the rich man passing through the eye of a needle drives the ranchers crazy."

"Wait a minute. The rich man doesn't pass through the eye of a needle."

"What are you talking about? The priest makes them pass through whenever he feels like it. He soaps them up, greases them, who knows, and the deal is that they pass through the eye of the needle and go to heaven. They tell me he gets standing ovations after his Masses."

"Barrante told me he's got two employees."

"Even so, he can't cope with all the work. Now he's going to spend the season in Punta del Este."

"You shouldn't be complaining then, since you get thirty percent."

"No, it was with Barrante I got thirty percent. This guy just pays me a fixed rate per diem, and just now he started paying me for Saturdays."

"If you could drive me to the traffic circle tomorrow, I'll be on my way."

"So soon? What's your hurry?"

"My partner's coming back from the casino."

"Look, I don't want to disillusion you, but that casino stuff seems like a pipe dream to me."

"What's the difference? It's still time to get going."

"Sure, but it's easier when you know where you're going. I'm going to La Paz, Bolivia."

"Do you mean it?"

"Why doubt it, Zárate? Goddamn it, things just have to get better for us!"

"I don't doubt it, but you're too fat to pass through the eye of a needle."

He slammed the door and walked out onto the patio. After a while, I heard him kicking the pump again. Through the window, I watched him straighten a wire he'd found on the ground and work it into a hole in the meter. In the twinkling of an eye, he found the switch and the gas began to pour out of the hose.

25 Salinas came back at dawn with two other men wearing cassocks, and Coluccini bawled them out for using the car without permission. They were so drunk and in such a good mood they didn't pay him any attention whatsoever. One of them, a very blond man, jumped up on the Gordini's hood and absolved all of us in rather coarse terms. Salinas first scolded him then helped him down, while the other, a short man with a big nose, took a ball out of the car and began kicking it against the wall of my room.

My sleep habits had reversed, so it didn't matter whether I slept at night or during the day. I crossed the patio to the water tank and took a bath while the others took off their cassocks, which they then set up as goals and boundaries. Several times, the ball rolled over the earth covering Barrante, but neither Salinas nor Coluccini said a word. The short man, who was fairly fast, called for the ball and organized the game in a gibberish that sounded a lot like Latin. Coluccini stood in the goal and even made a few diving stops. Each time he dove, he stayed on the ground for a long time, as immobile as a turtle flipped over on its back. The others laughed their heads off at him, not realizing that the fat man took advantage of his time on the ground to go through the pockets of their cassocks. After wallowing around three or four times he must have found something interesting because when I walked by him he told me in a low voice to get ready and wait for him in the car.

I got my bag and, to play things safe, walked over to the Gordini. After a while, the priests got tired, and the short one began vomiting against the door of my room. Coluccini gave them a friendly scolding and told them to go to bed while he picked up their cassocks, rolled them into a ball, and left them in the office. Salinas threw himself onto my bed and tried to shut up the blond who was declaiming an *ora pro nobis* as he pulled off his trousers and socks. The short man retched with his fingers in his mouth, and even though he could barely stay on his feet, he walked toward the office. Coluccini walked to the water tank unbuttoning his shirt as if he were about to wash, and signaled me to get into the car.

I opened the door carefully, praying for everything to go well, and jumped onto the seat. The fat man ran over and got behind the wheel, nervous and sweating. Before the others could react, he took off in reverse, scattering gravel. The short man heard the motor and ran out into the patio waving his cassock, shouting that his wallet was missing. Salinas, as if he'd seen the devil, leapt out of bed in his underwear. Coluccini just managed to miss the gas pump, went a few yards further in reverse, and then, just when the three of them were almost on top of us, threw it into first and headed for the road. Salinas kept up with us for a while, cursing, calling us thieves and bastards. As soon as we'd gotten a little way off, I stuck my arm out the window and gave him the finger. *"Vaffanculo!"* shouted Coluccini. "Go cry in church!"

The sun was shining directly into our eyes, so he asked me to get his sunglasses out of the glove compartment. Twice he tried to get the car into fourth gear, but the shift lever jumped, making a noise like massacred ball bearings.

"All right now," he shouted as he kissed his little medal, "let them set the dogs on me!"

"You always leave in a hurry," I told him, unable to hold back my laughter.

"I didn't have any other choice, Zárate. Just look at this." He handed me a sheet of notebook paper folded twice. I spread it out on the dashboard and saw a diagram drawn with a blue pen. It was a road that ended at a railroad station; an arrow pointed to two sets of tracks that joined together next to a signal light. "That's it, don't you think?" he asked me anxiously. "Isn't it the treasure map?"

"Looks like it. And what about the short guy's wallet?"

"A little traveling money. *Mascalzone!*" He slapped his hand against the steering wheel. "He paid me a fixed fare as if this were a bus! Was there a telephone back there?"

"Yes, but there's no danger. Is it the sacristy treasure?"

"Bound to be dollars. Or there just might be something more. Finally, God provides, Zárate. Never give up. Know what we're going to do?"

"Get thrown in jail. Sooner or later."

"No sir. When we dig up the treasure, we'll have fourth gear fixed and head for La Paz. Or would you prefer Santa Cruz?"

"It's all the same to me. But first I have to find my partner."

"Your partner! Who the fuck is your partner?"

I took out the photo Lem left for me and handed it to him. He took off his sunglasses, looked at the picture out of the corner of his eye, and handed it back, disappointed.

"Don't you have a more recent picture?"

"That's the only one he left me."

"Excuse me, but that guy's been losing since he was a kid." He pointed out the broken top Lem held in his hand. "You can't trust people like that, Zárate. Remember what happened to you in Venado Tuerto."

"I don't remember ever being in Venado Tuerto."

"You were. We'd just bought the tent, and you rented the

town square. You made a deal for twenty percent with the soldiers, and we ended up paying eighty and leaving the giraffe."

"Why did we have to leave the giraffe?"

"The colonel's mistress wanted it; you always made bad deals. That's why I'm telling you to watch out for that guy."

"I promised him."

"I hope you know what you're doing. Where do we start looking?"

"We don't have many choices. If there's a railroad station anywhere, it must be in Junta Grande. The priest couldn't go far on foot, right?"

"I used to drop him off at the traffic circle, right around here."

"You never went into the town?"

"No, I never wanted to risk it. Just think if the police ever made me open up my bags."

"That's where we've got to start."

"All right, but if they stop us, the bags are yours, Zárate. Like that time in Cinco Saltos."

"What happened to us in Cinco Saltos?"

"You took responsibility for the rent, and I got away with the circus."

"They locked me up, of course."

"You didn't have a cent, what could they do to you? After a month, they let you out."

"Fine. Now I'm a picture salesman on my way to Olavarría, okay?"

"Mar del Plata sounds better, Zárate. I mean, I don't know. I picked you up on the road and don't know you."

"Whatever you say. At the traffic circle, turn right. The map says it's a dirt road."

From time to time, a hare would dart out in front of us and then swerve off into the fields. The Gordini made pitiable noises, as if it was going to fall apart at any moment. Coluccini was a good driver, but every time he hit a pothole, he cursed in incomprehensible Italian. In a clearing, under a weeping willow, we saw the rusted remains of a Nash Rambler Ambassador: it was covered with moss and had plants growing out of the holes where the headlights had been. Then we came to railroad tracks, and the road curved to follow them. In the distance, we could make out the station and a handful of houses clustered around a plaza. Coluccini took his foot off the accelerator and told me to keep an eye out for cops, but as we got closer I realized there wasn't a soul left in the place. The streets were deserted and the houses abandoned. A forest of rioting leaves poured out of the plaza, covered the sidewalks, and jumped over the walls to enter the windows rotted out by humidity. We passed a National Petroleum Corporation sign which had fallen off a shed and then, opposite the church, we found the sun-bleached skeleton of a horse. Coluccini stopped the car and took off his sunglasses, a bit taken aback.

"Shit, and I was thinking about getting some breakfast."

We sat there for a while, looking around, not speaking. On the outside of what had been the town hall, the shield of the republic still hung, and someone had forgotten the bicycle he'd leaned against the wall. We got out and took a look up what had been the main street, which began at the station and died three blocks later at a wire fence running around a field. Coluccini pointed out a store with barred windows and looked through a broken pane.

"Nobody," he said. "They all went to Bolivia."

"Just like that?"

"Well then, you tell me where they are."

"Anyway, they ran out." I pointed to the counter where there was a bottle and several half-empty glasses.

The fat man pushed the door with his shoulder until the wood gave way and we could get in. There were as many spider webs and bats as you'd find in Dracula's castle. The plaster was falling off the walls, and the picture of Evita Perón, taken from a '50s magazine, had torn right down the middle. The overhead lights were covered with dust, and part of the ceiling, from which hung a wooden fan, had collapsed and was hanging even with our heads. A breeze would have been enough to bring the place down, and even the floor didn't seem very solid. The fat man, his lighter burning, went to see what was in back and then waved to me to help him get over the counter. I gave him a boost until he got his belly on the edge, and then he threw a leg over and jumped without worrying about what he'd find on the floor.

"Careful," I said, "there might be broken glass."

"No glass, but lots of roaches," he answered. "Give me the lantern; let's see if there's anything we can use for the trip."

I handed it to him, holding it with my handkerchief. There was still a lot of kerosene in it, and Coluccini held the lighter to it until he got a timid, yellowish light. On a table there was a pack of Brazil cigarettes (the kind my father smoked when he was young), a dirty glass, and an open bottle of beer. The beer had evaporated, but in the bottom of the glass there was a dark circle.

"I don't see any food, Zárate," said the fat man, slapping a bug walking on the counter. Next to the shelves was a mouse-eaten almanac whose final page was a Tuesday the eighth, with no indication of month or year. I also saw a photo of Troilo with his accordion and another of Oscar Gálvez handing out a Grand Prize. Standing on a chair, Coluccini dug around among cans of rotten cookies and empty wine bottles until he found two that were still full. He tossed me a bottle of gin and another of grappa, and before stepping down, he treated me to a juggling routine with some grimy glasses. Finally he dropped one, which broke on the floor, and it was then I thought I saw something escaping by dragging itself among the chairs.

"A virtuoso performance," I said.

"Remember? We knocked them dead down south."

Somewhere he found a corkscrew and began to pull the cork out of the grappa. I expected the cork to break, but he pulled it out intact. I again congratulated him, but he seemed slightly depressed. Then he handed me some red bank notes he'd found in a drawer.

"Look, these were the kind I used to buy the first bear in Santa Fé."

"Did you need a valise full?"

"No. Four or five were enough. Those were good times."

For a while, he concentrated on the bottle which, to judge by its label, was from another century. He sniffed the cork, touched it with his tongue, and then took a drink with his eyes closed and his nose wrinkled up.

"First rate," he said, passing it to me. At first I was a little apprehensive about drinking it, but the grappa was good, and I took a few swallows. Coluccini vaulted over the counter, knocked over some glasses, and landed next to me. He put the lantern on top of a can, brought over a chair, and we took turns with the bottle, leaning on a table where the blackjack cards had been left. "I'd just come from Italy," he told me, picking up a card. "In those days, even dogs ate steak. The bear was always sick because people would always give him bonbons and caramels. They even gave him chewing gum."

"Did you work with him?"

"Day and night. Until early evening in Retiro Park and at night in the clubs. We had two or three routines worked out, and I was putting money away. Then I bought the circus and got carried away. I don't know, I have to think about it."

"Think about what?"

"About why I fell apart, Zárate. You told me you hit bottom too, didn't you?"

"Like practically everyone else. Did you come to any conclusion?"

"I don't know. You went at the right time; you don't know what I went through. How ungrateful this country is with its artists, Zárate! I was famous. Once I was on the cover of *Radio Land*, I made tours through Uruguay and Chile, and then, where did I land? In the jungle; that's where I'm going. I could have set myself up in Spain when the General called me, but in those days, no one cared anything about Spaniards."

"Perón called you?"

"As a delegate from our union, yessir, he did. You insisted that I go, but I didn't want to get involved in politics. We got thrown in jail just the same."

"Don't get depressed. You're on the way to Bolivia, right?"

He was silent for a while, thinking perhaps about his disaster and how to survive it. He'd put his glasses up on his forehead, from which poured streams of sweat. Almost without realizing it, he picked up the other card that happened to be in front of him on the table and stared at the two of them distractedly. Suddenly he woke up, leaned back in the chair, and slid his glasses down on his nose.

"I'll stick with these!" he shouted in a much more enthusiastic tone of voice. I didn't think he was joking, so I picked up the cards in front of me. I fanned them and found a low number card behind the king of spades.

"I'll need cards," I answered, just to humor him, as I looked him in the eye. He seemed astonished by my audacity.

"Got anything to bet?" he asked, looking again at his cards as if he were afraid they wouldn't be there anymore.

"The trip, if you like."

"The one from before or the one coming tomorrow?"

"It's all the same to me."

"What did your partner bet?"

"Illusions."

"That's good. Bet yours then."

"I don't think I've got any left."

"Bet your friend's photo."

I felt Lem's photo in my pocket. I only had fifteen points in my hand, but I didn't feel like throwing it in.

"Once I fell desperately in love," I offered.

"Would you have killed yourself for her?"

"Well, you can see I'm still here."

"Then bet something better. It has to be a good memory. . . . A cruise, a desert island, I don't know . . . something I can tell when I'm in the jungle."

"When I was a kid, a ghost would appear to me. It came through the keyhole."

"Did it wear a sheet?"

"No, more like a cape, and it smoked quite a lot."

"The ghost smoked in your room?"

"Right, but it didn't leave any smoke behind."

"That would be a hard one to tell. I had a couple of good memories, but I lost them in Médanos. The priest Salinas won my last one the other night."

"You've got nothing left? Not even a tiny happiness?"

"I don't think so. The bear the newspaper was going to buy me . . . But who'd be interested in that?"

"You told me you'd worked together in Retiro Park, that people liked giving it bonbons . . ."

"That's right, but we landed in jail from time to time. That's not a good memory. What I've got left, if you think it's any good, is a girl from Chubut. She wasn't pretty and didn't go back to my room with me, don't get ideas."

"At least that's something."

"That day, everything worked right. Believe me, I'm telling you all this, but I'm not bragging." He half shut his eyes and leaned back, his cards tight against his belly.

"I think she must still remember, too. I saw her from above while I was walking the tightrope, and the air seemed electrified. She practically broke her hands clapping for me. 'I wish she'd come all the time,' I thought, and then I went into a double somersault, which is not my best move. It came out perfect, right down to the last twist. When I came down, Zárate shouted to me, 'Unforgettable, Fatty.' "

"What about the girl?"

"She was still there. Everyone else had gone, but she was still sitting there. Then I went over to talk to her, and when she looked at me I realized she was happy. 'Again,' she said, 'again, please.' What could I say? I went back up to the trapeze and went on for the rest of the night. Triple somersaults, corkscrews, swinging with streamers, everything . . . At dawn she stood up, crying, left a little handkerchief on her seat, and walked out. Do you know Puerto Madryn?"

"I need cards, Coluccini."

"I don't want to lose this memory, Zárate."

"Your ghost against my ghost."

He drank from the bottle until he choked and stood up coughing. I couldn't see him anymore; he disappeared into the darkness of the bar until I heard him knock over a chair and smash the bottle against the wall.

"I've got twenty, goddamn it!" he shouted from the depths of those ruins, and then he became as silent as a dead man to listen to another of his memories escape him. I had the five of clubs and the king and looked over at the deck to see where the dealer might have been.

"You win," I said, throwing my hand onto the table. Suddenly he started to laugh and appeared in the line of light, white with plaster dust, ragged, drunk, suddenly happy.

"Shit," he said, "I was scared to death."

27 Coluccini grabbed the gin and staggered out of the store, his shirt hanging out of his trousers, a sheet of filthy yellow newspaper stuck to his shoe. I turned off the lantern and followed him, but before I reached the door I again heard the noise of something slithering among the chairs. Back on the street, in bright sunlight, I felt calmer. Coluccini was making for the station, and he shouted to me to give him the map, although he was in no condition to tell the difference between a treasure and a locomotive.

I followed him through the weeds and picked up the sheet of newspaper the fat man had dragged out of the store. It was a page from *The Voice of Junta Grande,* but it too lacked a date. I saw an advertisement for an auction of young bulls and a column announcing the baptism of someone named Juan Floreal in the parish of Santa Lucía. The rest was illegible, except for a paragraph of praise for a lieutenant colonel who had swept the town clean of vagrants and beggars. I was reading that when Coluccini tripped over some thistles and began to laugh again, as if he were making fun of himself. I went over to help him, but when he saw me coming, he got up on his own, holding on to a post with a mailbox attached to it. That must have reminded him of something, and when he was on his feet again, the weeds up to his waist, he opened the mailbox and looked inside, as if he were expecting mail.

"You never know," he told me, pulling out a couple of discolored letters. The writing on them was as blurred as the newspaper print, and when the fat man tried to open one of the envelopes, he found that it had all turned into a solid lump no one could unfold. I tried with the other envelope, but it fell apart instantly, and I only managed to make out bits and pieces of a small, cramped handwriting.

"Since we've found a mailbox, why don't you send the Barrante kid's stuff off?" said Coluccini, his tongue thick, as he climbed out of the ditch.

I wasn't in the mood to argue, so I took the opportunity to write a few lines to Lem, informing him I was still in the area. Since I had neither paper nor envelopes, I wrote on the back of his photo. Before putting it into the box, I looked at it again and asked myself what he'd wanted to tell me with that message and if sending it back this way would offend him. Barrante's things all fit into a plastic bag I found in the Gordini's glove compartment. I wrote an imaginary address in Berazategui on the back of a cigarette label and left all of it in the mailbox while Coluccini tried to ride the bicycle forgotten in front of the town hall.

The hulk wouldn't move no matter how many times the fat man kicked the pedals. He seemed far away from that night in Chubut, but he was happy he hadn't lost the memory and was trying to show me some of his cheap tricks. I didn't want to see him fall again, so I strolled to the other side of the railroad repair shop. I found a signal light and a rail connection like the one Salinas had drawn on the paper, so I supposed it wouldn't be hard to find the treasure.

I called Coluccini, who was still going at it with the bicycle, and slipped down the railway embankment. A skunk ran through the weeds, leaving behind a stench that forced me to double back with my handkerchief over my nose. A flock of thrushes flew over the station, and I heard the hoot of a frightened owl. I saw some rats running away along the rails, but the smell of the skunk covered everything. I ran to a swamp, threw myself on the ground, and plucked some flowers to breathe in their perfume. From where I was, I heard the fat man's guffaws and turned around to see him. He was on the roof of the municipal building riding the bicycle, and he waved his arms until he was sure I was looking at him. He looked both impressive and ridiculous up there, naked from the waist up, with a tablecloth tied around his neck like a cape. He waved to an imaginary crowd, crossed his legs, which were very thick, around the forward part of the frame, opened his arms, and took off like a bat startled by sunlight.

As if in a dream, I saw him pass and forgot both the stink of the skunk and the priest's treasure. He seemed to float in the air, huddled over the black circles of the insane tires. It all took place in silence, with masses of tranquil clouds in the sky, under a round midday sun. I lost sight of him at the corner, when he passed over the Gordini, but he quickly reappeared above some cypresses and flew, casting a shadow on the roof of the station. There he seemed to stop, but then he took off straight ahead, making a turn around the church steeple. A flock of chimango hawks glided around him, and I stood up to watch him take a curve toward the outskirts of town. He used all the cables running from pole to pole, and leaning forward the way he was, he rolled along like a barrel. By now I understood the girl from Chubut, and when I saw him foul up on the last telephone wire, right over the railroad signal, I also understood why Zárate and the family had abandoned him. He glided a long way, sixty feet above my head, casting his shadow on the pasture, and after trying a flip, he smashed into a field of oats, right next to the mill.

Even then I heard nothing. He'd landed headfirst like a paper airplane, and the chimangos went on their own way. I turned my eyes toward the roofs of the town and felt that all the cables were still vibrating. For a moment I thought about doing what Zárate would have done—picking up the treasure and leaving—but it didn't seem like a respectable idea. I picked another flower to perfume my handkerchief and ran toward the mill.

28 As I crossed the wire fence, I remembered Lem's warning, but Coluccini was in a bad way and needed help. He was stretched out next to the pond, surrounded by cows, half covered up by the tablecloth he'd tied around his neck. He was trying to free his left arm, which was pinned under his back. I could see he was upset, but he smiled like one of the blessed, quite distanced from his dilemma—perhaps he was strolling through Chubut or walking the bear through Retiro Park. He gestured for me not to move him and then pointed into the distance, up high.

"I wanted to go up and see the countryside," he said, as if to justify himself.

"The wire was stolen, didn't you see that when we came into town?"

"What bastards . . . You saw me, didn't you? I had a tail-wind."

"I saw you perfectly."

"But you don't have anything to say to me?"

"What can I say? I never saw anything like it."

"And you never will again. Thanks for the applause."

I didn't remember applauding, but the truth was he'd earned it.

"You're very welcome. You were sensational."

"It's like music, see? You need an attentive audience."

"Does it hurt?"

"I think I threw my arm out of joint. Take a look, please."

I took him by the legs and pushed him over on his side so I could free his arm. His elbow was pointing forward, and it wasn't going to be easy to fix him up. Just then I remembered the night Barrante got the speck out of my eye.

"Has this happened to you before?" I asked, returning his glasses, which had fallen onto the ground.

"Occupational hazards," he answered. "You'll have to get it back into joint."

"If you tell me how to do it . . . A little gin would help, wouldn't it?"

"There was half a bottle left," he said, his eyes lighting up. "Think you can carry me?"

He held his good hand out to me and signaled that I should pull without being afraid. I braced my shoe on his so I wouldn't slip and began to lift him up. He grunted a few times, swore a bit in Italian, and when he could hold himself up, he grabbed on to me.

"There we are, Zárate," he whispered into my ear, "get going."

Coluccini moved with the elegance of a wounded deer. We staggered across the pasture, taking care that the cows didn't charge us. I held on to him tightly and supported his weight with my shoulder. There was still a bitter smell in the air, and he told me that skunk spray brought luck to travelers. Coluccini sounded on the verge of an asthma attack, and I stopped two or three times so he could catch his breath. When we got to the fence, I asked him if he felt he could pass between the wires, and from the look on his face, I realized I'd offended him.

"Just give me a lift and shut up," he said, leaning his shoulder against a fence post.

He put his other foot on the barbed wire, held himself steady on my head, and leapt into the air without giving it a second thought. Then he surprised me a second time: his hurt arm was hanging like a dead branch, but he could do wonders with the good one. No sooner had he landed than he grabbed a bush to regain his balance, spun on his heels, and slipped down the embankment on the seat of his pants. When he got to the bottom, he turned to see if I was following him, as if I was the Zárate who'd accompanied him during his acrobatic performances. I passed between the slack strands of wire and went to help him up.

"Is the treasure around here?" he asked as I dragged him along again.

"Under the railroad sign."

"You're going to have to drive for a while. We can spend the night in Pergamino, and in three or four days we'll cross the border."

"I already told you I have to meet my partner."

"If you insist . . . Reset my arm and then you can do whatever you like."

We walked around the station and then went out to the Gordini. Coluccini pointed to the place in the plaza where he'd left the gin, and I helped him sit down there. I handed him the bottle and we had a few drinks while he told me what I had to do to fix his arm. After a bit, he said he was ready and asked me to give him something to bite. I got some tree bark, carefully grabbed his arm and, as soon as he closed his eyes, gave it a sharp tug. He screamed and insulted me as if I were his worst enemy, but I was happy to see his arm was back in place. He emptied the bottle in one swallow, kissed his medal, and leaned back against a tree. We were sweating like bricklayers, and it took us a while to notice that near us, among the palms and bushes, Nadia's Citroën was parked. Sitting on the hood, smoking calmly, was the priest Salinas.

29   The three of them gave us a good beating, with clubs and all. Nadia stayed out of it, lying back on the grass, until she saw that Coluccini had lost his glasses and was defending himself with only one arm. That must have moved her—maybe she was still a little fond of me—so she

came over to stop the fight. The fat man was protecting himself
with the arm that was out of commission and howled each time
he was hit. The short man went wild and hit me over the head
with his club, but Nadia took out a revolver and began to shoot
into the air.

We all calmed down for an instant, and the truce gave Coluccini the opportunity to pound the blond, who'd done us the most
damage, with the bottle. He fell to the ground, shouted that he
was blind, and invoked the name of God. I wondered what I
was doing there, fighting men I didn't know, on the side of an
irredeemable scoundrel, but it wasn't the right moment to be
thinking about those things. During the confusion, while I was
twisting Salinas's finger, Coluccini slipped and the little man
tried to cut his face open with a piece of glass. Then Nadia fired
again, and we all stood still, as if the police had come.

"You again!" she shouted at me. "Why don't you behave
yourself?"

"I figured you'd be in La Plata by now," I answered, spitting
out the dirt in my mouth.

"Thieves, degenerates!" shouted the blond, trying to get to
his feet.

"All right, boys, everybody go home now," said Nadia,
pointing to the station.

That made me laugh. Coluccini looked at me suspiciously, as
if I were making a deal with the enemy. She was resplendent,
hair done nicely, fresh lipstick, looking younger than she did
the day we made love. I don't know if she remembered that,
because she pointed the gun at me just as she pointed it at the
others and again told us to get out of there. The fat man interrupted to say we'd had a bad accident and suggested we leave in
separate groups so no one could play any tricks.

"Io e il mio amico possiamo andare su . . ."

"Talk so people can understand you!" Nadia shouted.

"I was saying that my friend and I can go to the station, where
I have my car, while these gentlemen can go back to the road in
the Citroën. Is that all right?"

"No, because the Citroën is mine," said Nadia. "Are you the one who stole the map?"

"What map?" asked the fat man, who seemed sincerely surprised.

"Give it to me or I'll have you stripped. What were you doing on the roof?"

"I just went up to look around, that's all."

"To tell you the truth, ma'am," said Salinas, figuring he'd already lost his savings, "it's only a few pesos from the offerings. What we wanted to do was teach these thieves a lesson."

"Dollars, Father. You told me it was in dollars."

"Where would I get dollars?"

"From the ranch owners," answered Nadia, who must have known this story by heart.

"A priest never asks for money," said the short man indignantly, trying to help out his boss. But his voice sounded false, and Nadia slapped him across the side of his head.

"What the father said isn't exactly true," explained Salinas. "Sometimes we ask for bus fare."

"What bus, you good-for-nothing? I drove you around," Coluccini rebuked him. "I'll tell you where the money is, ma'am, but first get rid of these guys."

"Will you guarantee what he says?" Nadia asked me, a glimmer of friendship in her eyes.

"You can count on me," I said.

"All right, walk back over to the wire," she ordered the priests, and when Salinas started to argue she fired another shot into the air. A not very manly scramble took place. I jumped behind a tree, and the others ran toward the station. Coluccini didn't move, but from the expression on his face I realized something had gone wrong.

"I left the key in the car," he told me sorrowfully.

The priests now had the advantage on us. I was worn out, but they'd hurt my pride, and I wanted to see how the game would turn out.

"Do the others know about the treasure?" I asked the fat man.

"I don't think so, they're jerks."

"Where's the money?" Nadia insisted.

"Just behind the station," I told her.

"And where's the other one?"

"What other one?" asked Coluccini, annoyed.

"The sad one. The lost banker."

"He went to find a casino," I answered. "You put life back into him."

"Your partner has a bank?" asked the fat man, his mouth hanging open.

"And a brand-new Jaguar," I added.

"How much do you think there is?" asked Nadia, as she pointed to the corner where Salinas was searching the Gordini.

"A few thousand," said Coluccini. "If we don't hurry, they'll take it all."

"Get into the car," said Nadia. "We'll throw a scare into them."

I sat in the middle. There were just as many sausages and cheeses in the Citroën as before, and that brought back good memories.

"I knew we'd meet again," Nadia said to me.

"Once I was stretched out on the road, but you went right on by."

"No sense tempting fate. Have you learned anything during this time?"

"Very little. That people should stop when someone's hitch-hiking."

"That won't help us in Brazil."

"That helps everywhere," I said to her.

At the end of the street, Salinas and the others were barricaded behind the Gordini.

"Ram them, ma'am," said Coluccini. "Those little priests will run for it."

30   It wasn't like any of the car rammings I'd seen in movies. The Citroën was roaring, but it went so slowly the priests had plenty of time to take cover and throw whatever they could find at us. A stone smashed the windshield, and Coluccini shouted to me to find him something he could throw back. I dug through the provisions and handed him bottles, cans of pâté, everything I could lay my hands on. Then I realized Nadia had lost control of the car and that we were heading straight for the Gordini. But we didn't hit them head on because the Citroën was moving so slowly and at such a sharp angle to the Gordini. It was barely a scrape: we lost one fender and the two cars hooked their doors together.

Salinas ran off along the station sidewalk, and Coluccini shouted to me to cut him off. But it was too late. The priest climbed the hill, tripping over his cassock, and veered off toward where the treasure had to be. The other two handed over the keys without argument, and Nadia, who'd begun to lose her makeup, slapped the little one a few times, scaring both off into the fields. Night was falling, and the town was dyed a rather sinister ocher. I asked Nadia to stay and guard the cars while I went after Coluccini, afraid something irreparable might happen to him. I took a shortcut and grabbed him as he was going down the embankment, wild, on the verge of an asthma attack, his eyes popping out of his head.

"Get your hands off me, Zárate!" He pushed me. "That son of a bitch paid me a fixed rate!"

He could never forget that. Salinas ran into some tall grass and began to scrape the ground desperately. That money must have cost him many months of pulpit work going from ranch to ranch, so he wasn't going to give it up just like that. Coluccini tried to grab him by the arm, but he didn't have the strength, and the priest gave him a shove that put him on his back. It was then the fat man finally had an attack and began to foam at the mouth. Salinas picked up a shovel, smiled at me, and asked me how long it had been since I'd returned from Australia.

"I don't remember," I said, looking for something I could use to fight him.

"The fat man told me about you, Zárate. Get out of here or I'll split your head open."

Coluccini must have told him some of his partner's heroic deeds, and I felt obligated not to let him down.

"Is that stuff true about the rich passing through the eye of a needle?" I asked.

"Yessir, it is. There are many kinds of needles."

"Would you pass through, Father?"

"You've got to have what it takes," he said, pointing to the hole. "Are you going to leave or do you want another beating?"

"I don't know. I'm just having fun."

"Do you know how to get out of here?"

"Don't have the slightest idea."

"If you can get the car for me, we'll split fifty-fifty."

Coluccini was still writhing around convulsively on the ground, clutching his chest with both hands.

"We can't leave him like this," I said, pointing to the fat man.

"There's nothing wrong with him. Afterward, he'll just fall asleep."

"It's a deal." I spread my arms as proof of my friendship. "What would you think about our praying a little? We have so many things to ask forgiveness for . . ."

"Stop screwing around. You're not a believer."

"Oh but I am, I swear."

"God is a rather vague idea, did you know that?"

"That's good enough for me."

"You don't know how I envy you. Listen, I wanted to ask you something: do you miss things a lot when you're away?"

"A lot."

"I'm going to Madrid. What did you miss most?"

"This, for instance. The memory of all this—you couldn't give it to anyone. The stories you could tell about your lovers won't evoke anything for you, and whatever you tell won't matter in the slightest, not even to the most cordial manicurist."

"Nonsense."

"Sometimes you'll curse this memory, try to erase it, but I'll be there. The medium will be shooting off her gun, and Coluccini will be there on the ground until the day you die, Father. Aside from that, it's certain things will go better for you there. Those people have mountains of credit cards and always show up for appointments on time."

"So what do you want? Do you think I can spend the rest of my life in this hole? In a pit, up to my neck in shit?" He stood there for an instant holding his hand up next to his neck.

"It's your pit; it took you a lifetime to dig it."

"I didn't do anything. I spent ten years buried in a parish in Bernal, confessing thieves and whores, dying of hunger, preaching mercy, absolving people who'd find hell too small for them. What good memories of mine are you talking about?"

"Those very ones. I didn't say they were good. I just said they were yours."

"No, thanks. I'll make you a present of them."

He looked at the sky, which had turned overcast, and put something in the pocket of his cassock. Coluccini had either fainted or fallen asleep, stretched out on top of a sarsaparilla bush. It was getting dark, and on the other side of the station, everything seemed dead. Salinas pushed me with the shovel and told me to walk ahead of him. We walked up the embankment and turned toward the station. When I came to the street, I saw the cars and a horse that was wandering around loose. There was no sign of Nadia, but I knew she was waiting for us somewhere.

I waved to Salinas to come ahead, and when he was closer to me I pointed to a dot moving in front of the store.

"The medium's far away. Now's your chance," I said and threw the key into the street.

Salinas walked to the sidewalk without making a sound and picked up the key case. It was true that something was moving at the door of the store, but I couldn't make out what it was. The priest made a path through the valises scattered in front of the Gordini and sat down very carefully behind the wheel. He was probably imagining himself far away in Madrid, strolling up the Gran Vía or shopping in El Corte Inglés. But no sooner had he started the motor than Nadia appeared through the Citroën's broken windshield, pointing her revolver at his head.

"Get out, Father," she said, turning on the headlights. "Walk away and leave the offering on the ground."

31 The Citroën's battery must have been weak: the headlights were two feeble halos that barely lit up the grass. Salinas turned to look at me, then went and stood in the light. He crossed his hands over his lap and lowered his head as if he were in the Bernal parish church, humbling himself before the Creator. There was a certain charm about Nadia standing there in those black boots, her blouse tight, and the revolver in her hand. She stood behind the priest, frisked his cassock, and shouted to me to stop clowning around and come out of my hiding place.

I was tired and hungry and had conceived an idea of how the day should end. But I was worried about Coluccini and curious to know if he'd left Nadia any memories. I opened the door of the Gordini and took out a pack of Winstons from the ones Lem had left me. Salinas saw me light the cigarette and asked me for one, the way a man sentenced to death would, but there was no rancor in his voice. He would simply have to begin everything all over again, from Bernal to the ranches.

"It's a lot of money," Nadia said to him, putting the plastic bag on the seat of the Citroën. "How much is bus fare around here?"

Salinas gave her a frozen smile. He'd played and lost, like all of us, but he didn't want to talk about it. He shrugged his shoulders and looked at me again to find out if I was also enjoying his defeat. To calm him down, I winked at him, but I don't know if he could see me in the darkness. Nadia asked me where the fat man was, and I told her that he was flying over the roofs. Both of them looked up, but all they found was the gray sky, where a rather filthy slice of moon was shining through.

"He's a great artist," said Nadia, "he'll never have a cent, the poor guy."

I didn't want to shock her by mentioning the videos or the Bolivian jungle. I picked up the Citroën's fender and put it back in place, as if it were a piece from an erector set.

"Aren't you coming with me?" she asked.

"I'm not interested in Brazil. I've been outside the country for a long time."

"Tired of putting up with yourself, eh?"

"I wouldn't be of any use to you."

Just then Salinas ran off into the fields. I managed to catch a glimpse of his cassock as the wind puffed it out before he faded into the shadows. Nadia fired the revolver in no particular direction and then stuck it into a pocket.

"He was going to Madrid," I said. "Don't you feel sorry for him?"

"They're crooks. This country's full of people like that. Can you imagine? A priest . . ."

"You just robbed him."

"That's different. I'm a woman alone. . . . I've spent twenty years in these weeds stepping in manure, reading the cards in flea-bitten, run-down hotels. . . . I'm fed up with working for nothing, understand?"

"I can imagine. He felt the same way," I said and held out the treasure map to her.

"I don't have my glasses," she said.

"It doesn't matter. Will you remember me?"

"Yes, and don't get the idea that I have an adventure every day."

"No, of course not."

"Don't pass judgment on me for what happened one stormy afternoon."

"Don't worry; all the same, you aren't going very far."

"What do you mean?"

"Nothing you can't read in the cards."

"Destiny is wide open, do you realize that? A computer will never be worth what the eye of the astrologer's worth."

"There's less uncertainty, that's true. And everything falls apart on us."

"One day you'll explain to me how they work."

"If you've got the patience . . . Aren't you bringing Bengochea and his girlfriend?"

"When I'm set up."

I walked over and we exchanged a friendly kiss, just touching our lips. Then she left, with no windshield or hood, and at the last curve I heard another shot, which could have been either a farewell or a warning. The taillights glowed on the horizon for about ten minutes before they disappeared. It was then I knew I'd never see her again.

32 I turned on the Gordini's headlights and saw strewn on the ground the food Coluccini had thrown at the priests. I picked up all I could, threw it into the car, and went looking for the fat man. On the road, I found a bicycle wheel twisted by the crash.

"You're in a terrible mood," was the first thing I heard as I pushed aside the leaves of the sarsaparilla bush.

"How do you feel?"

"Terrific. Did the priest get away?"

"He did, but Nadia took the treasure."

"Shit . . . How much was there?"

"I don't know. Before she left, she said you were a great artist. Feel like eating something?"

"Did she really say that?"

"Those were her exact words. She also said you'd never have a cent."

"That remains to be seen. Did they steal the car on us?"

"No." I showed him the key. "Come on, let's wash up a little."

I helped him get up, and we walked to the pond by the mill. Fresh water had flowed in, so we took advantage of it and had a soak.

"I'm going to catch up to her," said Coluccini as he got dressed. "With that heap, she can't get far."

"She can't get hers into high, either," I mentioned.

"That means she's as good as in our hands. I have more faith in mine, as a car."

That time he walked without any help and even whistled the theme from *Zorba the Greek*. We gathered up the valises and sat down to eat in the car with the doors open. I leaned over to move

the mirror and saw I had huge shadows under my eyes and a big
bruise near my forehead.

"A great artist!" Coluccini repeated, barely able to chew.
"That woman knows things. If I had known she was watching,
I would have dedicated a double flip to her."

"Listen, I'm tired of hearing you sing your own praises. Don't
you have a grandmother?"

"My grandmother was hung in Perugia in Forty-three for being a Communist. I was a kid."

"Now you're going to tell me you fought in the war."

"In the Resistance. But I can't tell you anything about it
because I lost those memories in Médanos."

"Aha. And why can't you go back to Italy?"

"My father had a problem in Cosenza with an armored car,
and to save himself, he put the blame on me because I was already
in Argentina. He died in seventy-five, may he rest in peace."

"And you don't resent him for doing that?"

"No, things like that always happen. My mother threw it in
his face in a letter. At the time, she'd married a guy from the
weather bureau, and they went north to measure the wind."

"Nice family you've got there."

"At least I have one."

He stared at me for a while as he peeled a small salami, waiting for me to say something.

"I was in Italy working for Olivetti. Things were going well
for me, but when the military government fell, I came back. It
seemed worthwhile to me."

He was laughing out loud, but he suddenly pointed toward
the store. "Someone's in there," he said, turning out the overhead light. "Can you see?"

"I think I saw something a while ago. . . ."

"Are you sure the police didn't come?"

"I'm certain of it."

"Just to play it safe, Zárate, let's sleep out on the road. You
drive, because my arm is a little swollen."

The steering was stiffer than the Jaguar's, and the motor sent

hot air through a hole near the foot pedals. I turned on the high
beams and drove toward the store. The street was still deserted,
and I don't know why, but I again experienced all my childhood
fears. I began to turn toward the road, but Coluccini grabbed
my arm and pointed to a bush which had recently been smashed
down.

"A car passed through there," he said. "Take a look."

"It had to be ours or Nadia's—there aren't any others."

"We didn't go through there. That car had radial tires, like
the police."

I backed up a few yards and got out to investigate. There were
tire marks on the grass. I walked a few steps in the darkness,
trying to work up my courage, and tripped in the same place
Coluccini had fallen that morning. I was just about to fall headfirst, when I managed to grab the mailbox, whose door was ajar.
Using my lighter, I saw that Barrante's things and the message
for Lem were gone. In their place was an air-mail envelope from
Spain. Next to the stamp with the king's face, I recognized my
daughter's tiny writing. Under my name, she'd written only
"Poste Restante, República Argentina."

33 I went back to the car and placed the letter on
the dashboard. Coluccini expected me to open
it right away, but I had to be alone to read it. We followed the
railroad tracks and, in a short while, reached the traffic circle
with the restaurant. When the time came to decide which road
to take, I hesitated, and then Coluccini pointed to some glass
scattered on the asphalt: it must have belonged to the Citroën.
I drove in that direction.

We drove for more than an hour without taking a curve until
finally we spotted the first tree, which was next to a gate. I

pulled off the road, braking slowly, and stopped under the weeping willow while Coluccini nodded off leaning against the car window. Sometimes he snored, and when he woke up he told me about a twenty-story hotel being built in the jungle, near to where Che Guevara had been killed. He told me his mother would never have forgiven Che's killers, but I didn't believe a word he said and answered vaguely. Finally he fell asleep, and I turned on the headlights so I could get out and read the letter sitting on the grass. I opened the envelope trying not to tear it and found a single sheet of very thin paper. On it was a drawing of a little girl standing in the rain.

My daughter was in fourth grade, so I imagined she would pronounce *s*'s and *z*'s in the Spanish style. Argentine history— the First Junta, Belgrano, the campaigns in Upper Peru—would mean nothing to her. I told myself we were broken and would be for a long time. It sorrowed me that we'd plodded toward the abyss like blind cows, but at the same time I didn't want to be the only one to escape that destiny, which belonged to all of us. Suddenly the knot I felt in my stomach turned into nausea, and I walked to the middle of the road to throw up. The bushes were pushing up the asphalt and making their way through the cracks in the highway. I thought that one fine day the place would go back to being what it was once, pure calm under the sun and storms, with no trace of our fleeting presence.

I was getting so depressed that I turned out the lights and threw myself into the backseat to stare at the stars. Coluccini made a noise like a sawmill and refused to sell the tent to the preacher from La Boca. I tried not to pay any attention so I could fall asleep, but he became obstinate and pounded his fist against the dashboard, shouting he wouldn't, he wouldn't. Finally he gave up, but he'd hung on like the last of the Mohicans. If he did give up, it was only because he'd been abandoned. I followed the rhythm of his snores and also fell asleep, dreaming of unsolvable equations.

The numbers appeared scattered all over the screen, and I raised them to a power the program couldn't handle. I repeated the same gesture on the keyboard, infinitely, but the formula refused to establish an order of priorities, and the computer kept requesting that I verify the space available in memory. I was sweating because I was afraid the program was infected with some virus and that I'd be stuck forever. My friend from Rome came to help me with a map of Argentina full of incomprehensible formulas copied on the margins. We argued, but he answered me with snores as loud as Coluccini's, and every time I restarted the equation, the screen reconfigured itself and showed me a figure similar to the drawing my daughter had sent me.

I woke up late at night and went out onto the road to smoke a cigarette. As I walked along the asphalt, I thought I saw lights in the distance, but no one passed by there, and all I found were hopping locusts that hung on to my trousers. I went back, ate a piece of cheese, and relaxed in the seat. The first glimmer was appearing on the horizon, and I finally fell asleep, all at once and without nightmares.

34 When I woke up, I saw that Coluccini had made a fire under the willow and was roasting some sausages of rather dubious color. We drank maté until the leaves were used up, and then I stretched out on the grass to watch him. He figured out a way to pile up the coals with a stick and even managed to cook the sausages to a golden brown. We held them between twigs and opened two cans of beer the fat man had buried in the shade of the tree. I asked him how his arm was doing, and he moved it up and down to show me it was back to normal.

"This road goes to Cleveland," he told me. "Know anything about it?"

"No. Where did you hear that?"

"A little while ago, some kids in a Mercury passed by and told me that's where they were going."

"Cleveland, Ohio. That's in the United States."

"Ah! No wonder they seemed a little lost . . ."

"Know something? I have the distinct impression we passed by here before. Don't you remember that gate over there?"

"They're all identical, Zárate, just like the trees. I drove nine hundred miles with the priests and never knew if I was going north or south."

"Then it must just be my impression. Did you see anyone else?"

"No, but the medium can't be far from here. Any news?" He pointed to the car. "Good news?"

"Just news."

"Better than nothing, right? No one ever writes to me. Once my kid called me from Australia to ask why the fuck I was still here. He told me he was calling from a pay phone, can you figure that?"

"It's possible."

"He never called again. They must have caught him fooling around with the mechanism. He's really ingenious with things like that."

"Don't you miss your family?"

"Of course I do, but they admire Zafate and must be better off with him."

"Why do they admire him?"

"He's a champ. A winner."

"Aren't you?"

"I always got in the way. I don't like to get up early, understand? Once they all got the nutty idea of going to Japan. Know what time they get up in Japan? At six, they're already standing at attention, singing. I told Zárate: you go and send me a postcard. In the end, they went to Australia."

"Won't you have to be an early riser in Bolivia?"

"I don't think so. All you can do in the jungle is sleep and make money. I read it in a magazine."

"But Coluccini, there aren't even any ships in Bolivia."

"I can make do with very little. They say there's a lake and a gold mine the Indians keep hidden. Who knows: maybe I'll find the map."

"Do you feel all right? Want me to drive?"

"The problem, Zárate, is the revolver. That woman's armed."

"Nadia? Forget about her."

"I don't know. You told me it was a lot of money."

"I don't need it."

"We'll have to get some. Do you have good eyes?"

"Pretty good."

"Well, if you see the Citroën, holler. Let me take the wheel, you never miss a pothole. Go ahead and put things away."

I put the remaining provisions in order and checked the oil in the Gordini. It was so thin, I thought it was a miracle we hadn't thrown a rod. I told Coluccini, but he said not to worry, that he'd have the oil changed at the first service station. He said nothing more about it, put on his black glasses, and pulled onto the road.

He drove with one hand, giving the impression that he'd spent a lifetime on this calamitous blacktop. Before the sun went into hiding, we found the dirt road that led to the Shell station where we'd first met. Around a curve, still parked in the same place, was the Bedford loaded with watermelons. Right then and there I hollered to Coluccini, who put on the brakes and pulled up alongside the truck, in the shade, just as he'd done the first time. The driver was almost naked, as skinny as an asparagus stalk, and the sun had peeled off almost all his skin. The melons smelled rotten, but the man didn't seem to mind and kept his place next to the cab, his thumb in the air. All around him, the ground was littered with melon rinds covered with flies.

"Finito!" Coluccini shouted to him through the window. "Still haven't found a buyer?"

"No one ever comes by."

"How much did you say the load might be worth?"

"I haven't seen any prices for a long time, but ten million easy."

"Don't screw around, that's not worth shit."

The man pointed to the wheels tossed into the grass. He seemed disposed to go on with their previous conversation.

"If you pass through the town and have a tow truck sent . . ."

"Do you know Castelnuovo?" I asked.

He made a gesture of contempt and kicked a rind. He looked twenty years older.

"I would have gone with you," he said to the fat man, "but my wife's sick and I've got a kid in school. How are things over in Bolivia?"

"All right, but nothing to write home about," answered the fat man. "If I see the road service people, I'll send them here."

"I can't thank you enough."

"Did you see a Citroën without a hood pass by?"

"No. A few days ago I saw a bus that was playing music, but it went over that way." He pointed his finger toward the dirt road.

"Get in the shade," I told him and tossed him a cigarette.

He stared at me with disdainful rancor and slipped a filthy sack over his neck.

"Listen, if you see Castelnuovo, tell him from me that he can go fuck himself."

"Castelnuovo's dead," I told him.

I got the impression that was the first good news he'd heard in a long time, although he immediately began to have doubts.

"Weeds never die," he muttered.

"He died, I saw them bury him," I insisted, while the fat man pulled out, tooting his horn.

He was happy watching us disappear, a dumb smile on his face and his thumb pointing in no particular direction.

"I'd advise you to explain nothing," Coluccini reprimanded

me as he tried to engage fourth gear. "Out in the country, you never know who you're talking to."

"I'm sorry. Did you see I was right? We've been this way before. Bolivia's in the other direction."

The observation didn't please him. He looked at his watch and speeded up as if he had to get to a meeting on time.

"Have faith in me, Zárate," he said. "You know Colonia Vela, right?"

"A dog bit me there."

"Okay, we're going to fill up. This is our last stop."

35   I asked him if he had any money, and he passed me the phony roll he carried in his pocket mixed up with dust balls and broken toothpicks. The papers were wrinkled and wet with perspiration, but seen from a distance they looked like real bills.

"Impossible," I told him. "Around here they've got a telephone, a siren, and the police have a patrol car. Why don't we go back to the Automobile Club?"

"Get out and wait for me at the bar. No one should see we're together."

"No, Coluccini, forget it. Just think about how we look."

"We'll have a coffee in the plaza and then see how things stand. You're sure Bolivia's in the other direction, right?"

"I didn't say that. I lost my compass a long time ago."

He burst out laughing and dropped me at the corner where the Union and Progress Club stood. He went along the avenue at a speed much too noticeable for a town like that. I turned onto the main street, where the only shop window with a light in it was a pharmacy. From the corner, still far down on the cross street, I could make out the Esso pumps. The front of the police station was dark, and it must have been a century since the patrol car moved from the lot next door. The only patrolman I saw was barefoot, standing under a gas light, chatting with a man wearing gaucho clothes. It must have been the time of day when the electricity was shut off; there wasn't a soul to be seen. Crossing the street, I put my hand in my pocket to feel the roll Coluccini'd given me and pricked myself on one of the toothpicks. It occurred to me there was something I could do to make things easier if the fat man did get me into trouble. I walked by the police station again, crossed the street, and went into the lot where the patrol car was parked. I took a quick look around, and, seeing no one, broke a toothpick and crouched down next to a wheel, panting. I unscrewed the valve cap and pushed down on the valve with the toothpick. The tire instantly lost air without making much noise, the same as they had when I was a kid and we'd fool around after a movie. I made sure the toothpick was in tight and went to where it was darkest, walking as if I were taking a stroll.

The Gordini wasn't in the plaza, and I began to get worried. I decided to wait in the bar and walked in wearing the expression of a serious person. The Spaniard was still behind the counter and looked at me suspiciously until he recognized me. I said hello to everyone and, just to play it safe, sat near the door. In back, they were playing *mus* and *truco,* and some of the players turned around to look at me, as surprised as they would have been if a woman had walked in. The noise of the generator was the same as it was the last time, the man with the mustache was drinking his Cinzano, and nothing had changed position. I lit a cigarette and waited for someone to take my order, but no one came. I was getting bored when I heard the voice of the Spaniard, shouting to me from behind the counter.

"Well? How'd you make out? Did they refund your ticket money?" He spoke in a loud voice, and people began to pay attention to him.

"Every cent and at the current rate," I answered with the first words that came into my head.

"Hmm. And are you going to stay around here?"

"No, I just stopped off for a rest. The truck driver's still waiting for help."

"That's Castelnuovo's business. You could go see him . . ."

I smiled. Maybe that was a trick they played on all outsiders, an amusement or an intimate ceremony they'd amuse themselves with the rest of the year.

"Can I get a coffee?" I asked. It no longer mattered whether I could pay.

"And where did you get your refund, if you don't mind my asking?"

"In Triunvirato."

"That's funny. There's no station there."

It was a special day for me. I'd received a letter from my daughter and was happy to be on my way again. So I put my hand in my pocket, took out Coluccini's roll and waved it in front of everyone there.

"Forget the coffee. Bring me a whiskey," I said so that everyone would hear me.

The Spaniard stiffened. Seeing me put away the roll, he reached over for the black telephone next to the cash register. My heart was in my mouth, but I tried to keep him from noticing.

"Fuck the railroad!" he commented, speaking to the man drinking Cinzano, who never took his eyes off me.

"And what business are you in, if you don't mind my asking?"

"Computers."

"And can you earn a living doing that?" asked the Spaniard, who couldn't decide whether to serve me the whiskey or not.

"I work in the casino. I'm in charge of gains and losses," I answered, without thinking about what I said.

They exchanged interested glances, while the man with the mustache chewed a sausage daubed with mustard. Their closed lives, shot through with gossip and fear, made them hostile to the unknown. I wondered what the woman who'd turned Lem down was doing just then. Perhaps she was sitting in front of her TV watching a soap opera about the rich and famous. Or perhaps she was in bed, covered with creams, turning down her husband. I wished I knew where she lived so I could ring her bell and try to sell her a Bible or a raffle ticket for a benefit for homeless children. Then I thought she could just as easily be the coach's wife or the mother of the kid who'd brought me to the club, and that made me sad. I lit another cigarette and smiled. The owner had picked up the receiver and was waiting for a dial tone, but the Cinzano man was having doubts and grabbed his arm.

"Do you really work in the casino?" he asked.

"I'm on vacation now."

"And what did you say you did?"

"I make sure the house doesn't lose money."

"Dressed like that?"

"Of course not. In Mar del Plata I wear a suit and tie," I laughed. "Want to know why I'm here?"

"That whiskey: with or without ice?" asked the Spaniard, who was starting to get interested.

"A month ago, when my daughter got sick, I made a vow to the Virgin. Not that I'm very religious, but when you're desperate . . ." I looked at the man with the mustache, who had harpooned an olive and couldn't decide whether to raise it to his mouth or not. "So here I am, walking to the shrine of the Virgin at Luján."

They were both taken aback, staring at the floor until the man with the mustache gestured to the owner to pour him another drink. I was still waiting for my whiskey.

"Wait a minute: didn't you tell me you came by train?" the Spaniard objected, seriously upset.

"I'm not the kind of guy who can go around saying the Virgin brought about a miracle for his daughter. . . . After all, I work for Lotteries and Casinos."

"Lotteries too?" the man with the mustache jumped in.

"It's all the same department."

"God is everywhere and the Virgin as well," the Spaniard, who was beginning to be moved by the idea, interrupted. "Now, if you are going to Luján, I have to warn you that you've got a long way to go."

"Would you know which road I should take?"

"Well . . . you'll have to cut through Junta Grande, then Lobos, and from there . . ."

"Anyway, let me congratulate you," said the man with the mustache. "I don't know if I could do it, although for your own child you'd do anything. . . . Get him a drink, Francisco, it's on me. How is the child now?"

"She's just fine."

"Some very good priests came here to give blessings," the Spaniard intervened. "Ever since, no one's gotten sick."

"And your job," said the man with the mustache, "is to know the number that's coming up on the lottery . . ."

"No. To be honest, it's the other way around. I have to know which number is not going to come up."

"And a computer's good for doing that?"

"Ours is."

"Now I get it," he said, slowly coming closer to me. "And what good does it do you to know which number isn't going to come up?"

"If we didn't, the casino would go broke. I'm sorry, but I can't say anything more. It's a professional secret."

"I understand. For instance, I'd never reveal the opening price of the dollar to anyone. That's sacred information."

"You run a money exchange?"

"I wouldn't call it that. Only small bills circulate around here."

"There are no small bills," I answered, tasting the whiskey.

"I'm not really sure I understand what you do," the other attacked, "but if you know which number isn't going to come up, is that the same as knowing which number *is* going to come up? Is that it?"

"Not exactly. There's the order in which they come up. But

don't ask me any more about it because I can't tell you anything, understand?"

"Perfectly. Is it the same with cards?"

"Exactly the same. And thanks for the drink . . ."

"You're very welcome. My name is Maldonado. This trip to Luján: you're under an obligation to go on foot?"

"Well, I think so. . . . It's a vow."

"Because I've got my car here, and I could put you on the road. I mean, if the kid's better, why walk yourself to death?"

The Spaniard nodded agreement and poured more whiskey into my glass.

"I wouldn't want to put you out. Tonight I'll get going again."

"Just like that? Didn't you want to see Castelnuovo?"

Someone behind me began to laugh softly. The man with the mustache must have shot him a deadly look because the glee didn't last long. The Spaniard brought over a saucer of peanuts and another of olives.

"Don't you want to stay the night?" Maldonado asked. "People from outside are coming for a *truco* match, and a little support wouldn't hurt us."

"Look," I said in a low voice, "I've sworn not to gamble, and besides I'm not presentable."

"We can fix that up. What do you need?"

"I have to see the cards and make the calculations."

He took out a pocket calculator and put it on the counter. On his hand he had a wart the size of a grape.

"It doesn't have enough power," I said. "What I do is algebra, and for that you need a computer."

That took the wind out of his sails. The Spaniard hesitated before pouring me another drink, and this time he didn't give me any ice. They stared at each other for such a long time I thought they were going to call the police. Finally the Spaniard drifted off to the other end of the bar, and Maldonado began to shell the peanuts on the saucer. Without lifting his eyes, in a very low voice, he observed:

"Too bad. Tonight we're playing *truco* with some ranchers from Triunvirato who've just made a big deal."

"What can you do? Without a computer, it's hard."

"But I suppose it's not impossible. I'll get you a really nice suit, and tomorrow I'll drop you off in Luján."

"And why would you trust me?"

"I don't trust you. Beforehand, you're going to give me a demonstration sitting at a table here. What do you say?"

I didn't get a chance to answer. At that precise moment, the door opened, and Coluccini walked in wearing a gray suit with a red handkerchief that covered half of his lapel. He was freshly bathed and wore a perfume that was so strong it instantly changed the air. His bruises no longer showed, and he was so elegant he looked like someone else. He sat down on a stool, almost in front of the Spaniard, and carefully put his glasses down on the bar.

"*Eccomi qua,*" he said, taking out a pack of Winstons. "I want to get even. But this time we play with my cards."

36   I couldn't imagine where he found the suit and everything else. He didn't look like someone on the run from the police, but with men like him you just never know. He stared hard at me, banging his ring against the table until he managed to get the attention of everyone in the bar focused on him. I didn't answer immediately, because I wanted to figure out just what was going on. Maldonado grabbed the bottle and the seltzer and filled his glass without stopping us. The Spaniard was sweating, trying to look as imperturbable as a barkeep from the Old West, the kind who never ducks during a gunfight. In Italian, Coluccini said I'd fleeced him in Mar del

Plata and that he'd spent a week going from town to town to find me and get revenge. Then he mentioned Tandil and began to get tangled up in an impossible tale. I realized it was time to send him a few signals.

"I didn't bring any money with me; besides, I'm not interested in playing with amateurs," I told him in a scornful tone. "If I look this way it's because I'm walking to Luján. Something you'd never understand."

"*Miracoli!*" he exclaimed, slightly more on track. "In the Lions Club he performed some miracles!" He turned for the first time to Maldonado. "First he takes me with a straight, and then he draws three kings. Does that seem normal to you, sir?"

I made a discreet sign to Maldonado not to talk about me, and that seemed to put him into complicity with me.

"I'm absolutely certain you play with the help of a computer," said the fat man, "but now we're face to face, and I want to see if you can beat me again."

"I never saw a computer in my life," I replied, looking at the Spaniard as if asking him for help.

"This gentleman is a civil servant carrying out a vow he made to the Virgin," he managed to say, but Maldonado winked at him to disappear. Coluccini pretended to see nothing, but the part about my being a civil servant caught him by surprise, and I had to work to keep from laughing out loud.

"He's probably got the computer hidden in his car."

"I'm on foot," I commented. "That night I was lucky, that's all. Forget it."

"Sure, just like that. And the Jaguar, what did you do with that?"

Maldonado and the Spaniard stiffened, and that made me think Lem's car was not unknown in Colonia Vela.

"I lost the Jaguar to an even faster guy."

"Is that true?" Maldonado jumped, no longer knowing whom to believe. "Don't tell me you lost a Jaguar! . . ."

"Among other things. But I'd won it first."

"Okay, if you don't have any money, let's play a few hands just for fun. All right?"

"If you insist. . . . I don't have a cent."

"Go on," said Maldonado, who was now triumphantly ascending the pedestal of Argentine irony. "I'll stake you, up to a hundred dollars."

"Did you hear that?" I said to Coluccini. "This gentleman will back me up to a hundred dollars."

He hesitated a bit to gain time and pretended he hadn't understood me. I said it again in different words, trying to tell him he should let me win.

"A hundred you said?"

"I'll go that high and no higher."

"Okay, but with a fresh deck. Doesn't anyone speak Italian in this nation of pricks?"

No one said a thing, and that calmed him down. While the Spaniard arranged a table for us in back, and the other customers gathered around to watch, he told me he'd touch his tie three times whenever he had a good hand.

Maldonado handed me the deck, and I shuffled it a few times before passing it to Coluccini. As soon as he saw what the fat man could do with the cards, Maldonado became so nervous I had to signal him to calm him down. Coluccini embarked on a spectacle of prestidigitation worthy of a better setting. He fanned the cards as if he were playing the accordion, made them appear and disappear like the doves from a magician's top hat, and before giving them back to me, he created a vast castle along the full length of the table. I congratulated him while everyone else applauded, and I thought that with just what he'd done there, he could have made his fortune in Australia. The first bet, five dollars, and another for twenty, he won, but after that I gave him a thrashing that shocked everybody in the bar.

He'd lost two hundred dollars when he asked for a time-out so he could take a shower. I had no idea where he'd gotten the money, but he paid me religiously, and Maldonado's eyes glittered as if they were made of glass. Coluccini said good-bye to all of them in Italian, but since he was leaving in defeat, they didn't bother to applaud, and that must have affected him a little. He was a broken-down artist in search of his last ovation. I followed him with my eyes until he opened the door and disappeared into the darkness. Maldonado was exultant, convinced that I could pick out the right cards in all the decks in the world. He told the Spaniard to pour us another round, and when the curious bystanders went back to their tables, he took fifty percent of the winnings.

"Look," he said, "tonight there's a dinner, and we're going to make up a six-player table with the guys from Triunvirato in the Rotary Club. Once a year, when there's a big sale, both towns put up their best players and bet a lot. There's a little party, the ladies come, and everything's nice. But we haven't beaten them for three years, and people are nervous. If you come in with us, you'll make some money, and tomorrow I'll drive you to Luján."

"But you saw I made a deal with the Italian."

"Put it off until another time."

"What kind of money are we talking about?"

"You don't have to worry about that. We put up all the money that goes into the bank. I'm offering you five hundred."

Then I began to understand why Coluccini was still obsessed with the fixed rate Salinas paid him.

"Anyway, you're not risking a thing," he added.

"And if someone turns me in?" I protested. "I work in Lotteries and Casinos and could lose my job."

"Go on! Who knows you? Did I ever ask you what your name is? I'm not even sure that what you told me is true."

"Then why don't you use someone else? There must be some good players around here."

"There are, but for three years now we haven't had any luck."

I looked at him, trying to gain time before answering. The Spaniard came and went impatiently, and from the smiles and attention he lavished on me, I deduced he'd sunk a lot of money in the pot.

"Naturally," Maldonado said, "the clothes are on us, a present you can take away with you."

"Don't try to make deals now. Remember, I won a Jaguar once."

"And then you lost it. That's life."

"Five hundred isn't much."

"What more do you want? Besides, I have to meet with the Rotary Club guys to see if they approve the idea."

I had to know what Coluccini's game would be, but in the meantime, I told myself I wouldn't lose anything by accepting. I asked Maldonado to sweeten the deal, and he agreed to six hundred plus the clothes. To calculate my size, he called the Spaniard over. They both measured themselves against me, back to back, and concluded I was the same size as someone named Roch, who would also be at the dinner.

"All right, if anyone asks you who you are, you tell them you're the subdirector of the bank and that your name's Rufino. Can you remember that?"

"Rufino, sure. Do I have a family?"

"Of course. A wife and two kids. Later I'll introduce you to the lady, because you have to be seen with her at the Rotary Club. I can't put you up in the hotel because the Triunvirato people are there. Check into the boardinghouse across the street, and I'll have the suit sent over right away. Get a good shave and clean your nails."

"And what do I do with the wop?"

"Call and tell him you're sorry. If he makes trouble, tell me, and we'll have him locked up for the night. The chief of police has a lot of cash invested in this. He'll be with us at the table."

37 I called Coluccini and told him to come over to the boardinghouse right away. He'd checked into the only hotel in town under an assumed name, but all I had to do was begin to describe him and they instantly connected me with him. He must not have been alone, because he spoke to me in Italian, pretending he barely knew me. I didn't want to say too much either, because there were two gauchos sitting nearby drinking maté and playing dominoes.

"Wait for me in your room, *ingegnere*," Coluccini said, hanging up without letting me finish.

This boardinghouse was better than the one in Triunvirato. It had a wardrobe, a sink with a mirror, a shower, and even a clean towel. Coluccini walked in and immediately proceeded to urinate in the sink. He closed his fly, and then produced a toothbrush and a disposable razor, which he tossed onto the bed. He was positively elegant, with new shoes and a different shirt from the one I'd seen him wearing in the bar. He looked much younger, and no one would have imagined him a human wreck lying in the weeds. I asked him where he got all that, and just as he was about to tell me, a country man knocked at the door to tell me he was bringing me the clothes "sent by Dr. Maldonado."

"Well, Zárate, I see you didn't lose any time either," said the fat man when the hick was gone.

"Rufino. My name's Rufino now, and I'm subdirector of a bank whose name I don't know."

"The Cattleman's Bank. Any idea how much we can make on this?"

"They promised me six hundred dollars, but it means taking a big chance."

"So they're giving you a fixed fee . . . ," he said with a sigh of disillusionment as he sat down on the bed, pulling up his trouser legs so they wouldn't split. "Want to know the good part? The Triunvirato people don't have a cent. They can't even pay the hotel bill."

"You know all about what's going on tonight?"

"Of course I know. Why do you think I went to the bar?"

"What's your game, Coluccini? Who loaned you all those clothes?"

"Your partner. He left a whole wardrobe in the hotel."

"Lem? Be serious now, and stop screwing around."

"He fleeced the ranchers, and now things are looking very grim. He took off with at least a hundred thousand greenbacks."

"I don't believe a word you're saying. Where did you say you ran into him?"

"Over where they give away the food to the poor people. I went to hide the car and found a Jaguar. Right away I thought, 'This guy has to be Zárate's partner,' and there he was, chatting away with the priest. He's pretty weird, if you don't mind my saying so. When I told him you'd come with me, he asked me to tell you that everything had turned out fine."

"Why did he give you the suit?"

"Because I asked him for it. I told him we were going to try our luck here and that we wanted to get to Bolivia as soon as we could. That's when I found out he'd skinned the Triunvirato guys. 'Tell him everything turned out fine, and that my job's done,' he said."

"Anything else?"

"Isn't that enough? Oh, right . . . that you shouldn't cross the wire or something like that, I don't really remember. The thing is, he gave me a valise with all kinds of stuff in it. A good thing I looked through it, too, because the clothing isn't the kind they sell in stores, that's for sure. Look, I can't button this jacket, and I had to open the seam of the pants in the back— but you can't tell, can you?"

"Let me see."

He turned around and raised the flap. It wasn't a bad way of getting around the problem: he'd opened the seam so the trousers would fit over his potbelly. The jacket covered everything, but if he ever bent over, he was dead.

"This is our big chance, Zárate. The Triunvirato men can't put off the game, and at the same time they can't lose because they don't have any money. Understand?"

"More or less. They can pay with a check."

"Pay a gambling debt with a check? What kind of excuse could they make up? That someone they didn't know passed through the hotel and plucked them clean? They'd look like fools. This party is a tradition that's been going on for eighty years."

"How do you know all that?"

"Because I moved into the hotel. Your partner left some money for you."

"You connected with the Triunvirato people there?"

"Yes. They're a pretty soft bunch. They gave me the money you won off me. Tonight one of them's going to have a heart attack or something, and I'm going to take his place."

"The other side might protest."

"No, I'm doing ranch business in Triunvirato, and everyone saw you destroy me in five minutes. Besides, if they start in about me, we'll ask about you. But that's not going to happen; this is a gathering of gentlemen. Two families that come together—like a birthday party. If it weren't that way, they'd be playing poker."

"So what's your plan?"

"Don't play dumb. You know you have to lose."

"No, Coluccini. I'll never get out alive."

"Come on, get ready; we don't have much time. The Triunvirato people know we're making a deal, but the men from this town will think I came to continue the game in the bar. You'll beat me again, okay?"

"Don't go so fast."

"How much do you think there is in the bank?"

"They didn't want to tell me," I answered, as I made my way

to the shower. The water was cold, but it did me good, and I stayed under for a while, hoping it would ease the pain of my bruises. Then I shaved with the razor and shaving soap Coluccini'd brought. While the fat man went on talking, I thought maybe I would have done better going with Nadia.

"You're not listening," Coluccini grumbled. "Don't you want to know how much there is in the bank?"

"It won't be of any use if they throw me in jail or shoot me. The chief of police put in a lot of money, did you know that?"

"They put together ninety thousand dollars."

"How much?"

"This time our fortune's made, Zárate! We'll skip Bahia and set ourselves up in Miami. Come on, get dressed, let's see how the suit fits." He took out a paper napkin and unfolded it on the night table. "Don't worry about details, I've got everything under control."

I put on the shirt and the trousers and went over to see what he was talking about. It was a drawing of a house that faced the street. He loved plans. I didn't believe a word he told me, but I had nothing else to do and so let myself be carried along by his enthusiasm.

"See? This is the room where we play cards. In this other one we have dinner. The men's room is here"—he put his finger on a square marked with an X—"and this is the kitchen, which has a sort of window or ventilator that opens onto the patio. Got it?"

"Yes, but I'm not convinced." I tied my tie and turned around to look at myself in the mirror. I hadn't looked that well for a long time.

"The first small pot your side wins, and the second we win. When a good pot comes up, I'll deal thirty-two to one of you and thirty-three to a man on my team who's captain of a corvette. Anyone holding thirty-two is going to start betting."

"You know how to handle the cards?"

"If I'm dealing I do. Cut the deck deep each time you see me touching my tie." He handed me a comb and stood on one side of the mirror. "But be careful, and every time your side gets a good hand, tell me. You could touch your watch, for example."

"Mine broke a long time ago."

"Your shirt cuff, then. Your right cuff, if it's just a good hand, your left cuff if it's a *truco*. I'm going to do the same thing a couple of times so you can guess my hand and look good, okay?"

"I don't like it. Six hundred dollars is a safer deal."

"Who says that if we go at it man-to-man, your side's going to win?"

"What do I know? Show me that plan again."

"When the game breaks up, we'll stand up to say good-bye to each other. I'll talk to them, and you pretend to go toward the bathroom, but instead just keep going to the kitchen. Open the window and jump out. If it's locked, go through the bathroom. After that, you jump over a wall and you're in the street. The car's on the other side of the station, behind some hedges, right opposite the chapel."

"I know the place."

"From when?"

"From when the dog bit me."

"Come by with the car and pick me up in front of the hotel."

"Who says they'll pay you?"

"Who says I'll have to be paid? Do I look like a sucker?"

"I don't get it."

He took out his wallet, where he had another fifty dollars and a foreign check with more colors on it than a garden in bloom.

"See? Thirty thousand, which is our share. A Miami bank, as it should be. You can't fool around with this."

"It's unsigned."

"It's only logical. When the thirty-three comes up, they'll sign."

"I'm sorry, but I still have some doubts. Suppose they don't sign."

"You're going to be jumping through the window. Then I can tell the truth, that you were playing to lose."

"And they'll all come running after me."

"Zárate, it can't happen. Just imagine the scandal it would cause. One town would declare war on the other. No, this is a gentlemen's affair. For the Triunvirato men, the important thing is to get out of a jam. Understand? Any more doubts?"

"Yes: that window or ventilator or whatever it was in the kitchen, won't it have bars on it?"

He started to laugh and stood up carefully so he wouldn't split his trousers. "Your partner is right. You're an incurable pessimist."

38 Before he left, Coluccini called over the gaucho and asked him to change his fifty-dollar bill for small notes. Right then and there, the hayseed reached into his baggy pants and pulled out two twenties and a ten. The fat man pretended to pay me and did not miss the opportunity to warn the gaucho never to gamble with me unless he wanted to lose his business and everything else he owned. They walked out together, and I was left alone in the room. The clothing Maldonado sent wasn't in the latest fashion, but it was almost new and freshly pressed. Obviously he didn't consult with anyone about his decisions, and if Coluccini's plan did work out, he'd have to make his escape right behind us. I sat down to think about the plan's weak points and found so many that finally all I could worry about was the kitchen window and the skylight in the bathroom. I told myself that even if we managed to get away, no matter how much of a lead we had on the police, the patrol car would follow us all the way to hell. For a second I was tempted to give it all up, but Coluccini stuck his neck way out this time, and it would have bothered me to leave him swinging in the wind.

I asked one of the locals for paper and an envelope and wrote to my daughter. I told her things were going well for me and that I was happy to be back; I also wrote that I was working on a project for a computer hook-up among all the power plants in the country, that I was traveling a lot, and that was why my letters got lost. I added a p.s., promising to visit her as soon as my contract was up, and then I left the letter with the local so he could mail it when the post office opened. Just then a blond man walked in, his hair slicked back with pomade. He must have been the local heartthrob. He was wearing a double-breasted suit and a striped tie he straightened in the vestibule window. He stood there admiring himself for a minute until he figured out which one I was and told me he'd been sent by Dr. Maldonado to introduce me to the woman they were going to pass off as my wife. I told him I was ready. We got into a mud-spattered pickup and drove to a brick chalet with a charming garden. On the way, he winked at me a couple of times and warned me that my wife was his sister and that the whole town was depending on me.

The woman was a short, fat, freckled blonde; she wore a wedding ring and looked as if she'd put on her finest outfit for the Spring Party. Her husband was sitting in an armchair, wearing boots, and from his expression I could see he didn't like the joke one bit. The first thing he did was ask me why I didn't have a wedding band. The leading man noticed the detail and got frantic, but he settled matters by ordering the husband to lend me his. What followed wasn't very honorable for the husband, but the blonde took it all as a joke or revenge and began to laugh. The leading man went to the bathroom and came back with soap for the husband's finger. The two of them began to pull, but the ring wouldn't budge.

The chubby little woman was having a great time, and I got the feeling she didn't enjoy life. She couldn't have been more than thirty-five, but I was sure she slept dressed and didn't know anything beyond this town and the guy who smelled like manure. Finally the ring slipped off, and she put it on my finger as if with that gesture she could begin things all over again. For a minute, I was sorry I had to escape through the window. I asked her what her name was and then, to mortify her husband, told her I'd been divorced in Europe, when I worked for the casino in Monte Carlo. Her brother, who paid no attention, said that Alicia and I had to leave right away for the Rotary Club, and took a brand-new deck of cards out of his pocket.

"This is the condition they'll be when you start playing," he said.

He caught me off-guard, but I made no move to grab them. I told myself that they may have wanted to test me again, so I simply would not react. I took off my jacket and told him to put the deck on the table while I stretched my fingers to crack my knuckles. Next to the cards there was a prescription pad from a veterinary establishment. The three men looked at me as if they expected a miracle, but the only thing I could think to do was to flip over a few cards and jot down a few undecipherable logarithms on the pad. I asked the husband to cut the cards and pretended to carry out a long cube-root operation.

"That's good," I said, "but if the order of the cards changes, I can lose."

"Maldonado took care of everything," said the blond, looking at his watch. "If it's all right with you, you can get going now. And Alicia, keep your trap shut, right?"

She lowered her eyes, and even if it was for only a second, she must have erased both men from her existence. She stood there waiting, her purse in her hands, wearing that flowered dress which hung below her knees.

"Park at the entrance, engineer. My brother will show you where."

I shook hands with the husband, who looked away, and opened the door of the Peugeot so she could get in first. She was so surprised by the gesture she didn't know what to do until I took her by the arm. Then she understood that it was like the movies: she returned my smile and sat down as elegantly as she could.

"At the corner, turn right," she said, her voice suddenly fading.

I turned on the lights and pulled away slowly. As soon as the house disappeared from the rear-view mirror, she lit a cigarette and leaned back against the window.

"Were you really in Monte Carlo?"

"I really was. They have a beach and a prince."

"So what are you doing here?"

"Life's little tasks."

"You're an imposter, right?"

"Aren't we all? Are you interested in philosophy?"

She burst out laughing and told me to slow down, that she was ashamed of what she was doing.

"At least over there in Monte Carlo they make fun of everybody."

"Don't be so sure. Even the prince has his problems."

"But there are princesses, and he can choose. Drive around the block, please."

I turned onto the main avenue, passed by the pharmacy, and stopped at the corner of Castelnuovo's street. There were lots of dogs barking at us, but I immediately recognized the growl of the one that had bitten me.

"Know what I'd do in your place if I thought I couldn't choose? I'd go to bed with the priest, who's a nice person. Or with the guy who coaches the kids in the club, I don't know what his name is. If you don't do that, then become a teacher out in the country or get your husband's car and money and move away, but don't tell me you can't choose. You of all people. Just admit you didn't have the courage, and that's that."

"You don't understand," she said, wounded. "Men always ask for too much. Let's go, please, it's getting late."

We drove six blocks in silence, and when I parked in front of the Rotary Club, she was as stiff as an iron rod. The guests were already arriving, and a man standing at the door was greeting them.

"I have a girlfriend who met a man from a different world

who offered to take her away with him. He was fed up with everything and was going nowhere. First she said she would and built up a lot of illusions, but later she realized she was only fooling herself."

"That's a lie," I interrupted her. "You were afraid."

She looked at me and huddled against the door, squeezing her purse in her hands.

"And what do you know about it?" she snapped back disdainfully.

"I was there," I said. "He was satisfied with a smile and a distant gesture, remember. Now get out, ma'am, people are starting to stare."

39 The man at the door bowed to us exaggeratedly. As soon as we entered the ballroom, a waiter hurried over to offer us hors d'oeuvres and everyone greeted me as if I were an old friend, not forgetting to mention my name so the Triunvirato people would see I was a member of the family. Alicia looked a bit upset, but she stayed right at my side like a good wife. They all had their best clothes on, the lights in the chandeliers were all burning their brightest, and on the walls there were paintings of Argentine horses and photos of champion bulls.

They introduced me to the Triunvirato men, who were also with their wives, but no one mentioned the game. Coluccini, with a cute little blonde hanging on his arm, was speaking an incomprehensible jargon, and when he shook my hand he called me *onorevole*. The priest was the same one I'd seen at the funeral. He was wearing a summer cassock and seemed to agree with everything being said about exports and kinds of exchange. We chatted for a while about vague things, and I understood that for them this was a very spécial day, because they were making intimate jokes and allusions to people who weren't worthy to be there. An old man who seemed half deaf insisted on calling me Rufoni instead of Rufino; it created a certain uneasiness until his wife dragged him off to talk to the police chief.

Maldonado walked in just before dinner was served. He said hello to everyone and went to the other room to drop off a briefcase that must have held the money. When he came back, he sat down opposite me, and since I stared at him, he nodded very prudently that everything was going well. A tipsy man asked Alicia how her husband was, and she answered that he was fine. At the same time, she looked at me with a broad smile and took my hand—right before everyone's eyes. The Triunvirato men pretended not to listen and seemed better trained, perhaps because there were only a few of them and because they were afraid, although I thought I could detect Coluccini's style in their performance. I tried to speak as little as possible, paying close attention to how the others behaved at the table. The most decorous was the ship captain; he had some experience in handling forks and knives and was the one who cut the melon from the rind most delicately. The others cut as best they could, and some even put the prosciutto on their bread. Alicia was mournful and ate almost nothing. She had to explain something to me, but she was afraid of ruining her associates' plan.

Before dessert was served, she got up and walked out through a corridor that wasn't in Coluccini's plan. It was then I realized his drawing was badly done. Just to be sure, I took careful note of where the waiters entered and exited, calculated the height of the windows that faced the street, and when Alicia came back with her makeup redone, I asked her where the bathrooms were.

While we were eating our ice cream, she passed me a note under the table and asked me in a low voice if I had seen her friend and the foreigner with the Jaguar together. I said I had, without adding anything because Coluccini was looking at us out of the corner of his eye, nervous about our conversation. She leaned over my back, pretending to ask the priest about taking up a collection for charity, and without waiting for his answer whispered in my ear: "What's he like?"

"Forgettable," I said.

While coffee was being served, Maldonado stood up to express thanks to the Triunvirato Rotary Club for visiting and to praise the government to the skies. It was a short, not very enthusiastic speech, but there was lots of applause. Then someone from the other team spoke, saying pretty much the same things. At the end, Maldonado invited us to a meeting to discuss the tendencies of the farm economy, and those of us who were going to play cards stood up. When he saw that Coluccini had also stood up, Maldonado looked at me to find out if I still had the nerve to take him on. I signaled back that I did and walked over to return the car key to Alicia.

"And she, what's she like?" I asked her.

"Unforgettable," she whispered through a contained smile.

Just then Maldonado took me by the arm and brought me along with the others.

40 The first game we won easily, and in the second I made an excellent show of myself several times, thanks to Coluccini's signs—he would tell me if they had the ace of spades or the ace of clubs. We were tied in points, and then the police chief, who was on my team, drew twenty-eight. The fat man warned me he had twenty-nine hearts, and prepared a slam. I told my partners we shouldn't challenge, but the police chief argued that it was only a matter of three points and that the Italian was a show-off who didn't have anything. I looked at

Maldonado and told him that in my opinion they had better cards.

"There are twenty-nine hearts floating around," I said, as if to myself.

The chief insisted that he was confident and without asking any more advice, shouted "Twenty-eight here, goddamn it." We all looked at Coluccini, who made a domineering face as he tossed out the four of hearts.

"Twenty-nine's better," he said as he turned rather aggressively toward me: "Did you guess or did the computer tell you, *ingegnere?*"

I didn't answer, but I realized that Maldonado and the chief had just learned a lesson and were looking at me as if to beg my pardon.

"That way we're just going to give them everything," I protested, and the lost hand caused us to lose the second game. So we had to play the tie breaker. In point of fact, I didn't go for a small slam I drew almost at the end, and whenever Maldonado and the chief had strong hands, I communicated it to Coluccini by touching my shirt cuffs, as he'd asked me to do.

The toughest part came during the tie breaker because the chief was really drawing good cards, and no matter how much I signaled the fat man, we started piling up points; the Triunvirato team began to get nervous. Maldonado was convinced I could guess how things would turn out, and since he was very drunk, he started to show off and make obscene comments. The chief also had a fiery style, and the only thing our opponents could do was weather the storm of our wins. I dropped a few hands so the difference wouldn't be so great, but not even that helped.

We had eight hands and led them by four, when Coluccini shuffled the cards and gave me a look that said the time had come. It was time to cut very deep and pray that the cards would come up as he wanted. Maldonado never stopped making jokes in poor taste and mocking both the fat man and the Triunvirato player who'd responded to his speech at dinner. The third player on the Triunvirato team was the ship captain, who never seemed to have seen the ocean but who inspired respect because of a scar on his forehead. He was quite old and claimed he'd had the privilege of firing a cannon at Perón in 1955. Despite those credentials, when he lost a big hand, Maldonado began to smoke his cigarettes and call him "sergeant." The atmosphere was tense, and I watched Coluccini's hands as he pretended to shuffle and took the measure of everyone at the table out of the corner of his eye.

I cut just as he'd shown me, and the cards began to fall at top speed near the coffee cups. The first one I picked up was the ace of clubs, which came with a two of spades. I looked up and saw the chief was moving his beard to tell me he had the seven of hearts. I winked that I had the ace and set everything up perfectly. When it was my turn to bid, I asked the chief how far he wanted to go.

"I'm holding the queens," he said. "I don't know, what do you think?"

"This is starting to get on my nerves," I warned him, realizing he had the thirty-two Coluccini had told me about.

"Open the bidding to see what happens," he said.

"Four spades," I said, almost whispering as I took out a cigarette. The ship captain stared at his cards, but Coluccini, who'd turned bright red, slammed his fist down on the table and, dropping his Italian, said, "We'll just see about that, goddamn it!"

The chief's eyes began to glow, but he didn't give up hope yet. He looked at Maldonado and then asked me what the Italian could have.

"There are two big cards out there together," I said. "If you don't have them, start worrying."

"Stay calm, *ingegnere*," Coluccini answered me, and then, without giving me time to do any play-acting, he faced the sailor with a triumphant grin.

"You're fucked, captain," he shouted, dragging out the syllables. "Let's try thirty-two and double them!"

"What kind of card-playing do you call that!" complained the

Triunvirato man who'd followed up Maldonado's speech. Then he tossed his cards on the table as if he were giving up.

"Not so fast, buddy," Coluccini stopped him. Now he began to make up songs while he fiddled with his cards:

> In my hand I hold a mystery
> in my heart a secret pain,
> don't wave the white flag yet, my friend,
> 'cause I think we've won the game.

At first they couldn't believe Coluccini's thirty-three but he had an air of high seriousness to him, as if he were gathering up the broken timbers of a shipwreck. I told myself it was time to get ready to jump out the window, so I put away my cigarettes.

"He's just fucking around," stammered Maldonado, but he was definitely unsure of himself.

"The gentleman pulled out the thirty-three," the ship captain insisted sweetly, while the Triunvirato speechmaker went back and counted the points. The chief looked at me in rage, as if he were demanding an explanation.

"I told you there were two big cards outstanding," I said.

"And what advice do you have for me now?" he asked, from the depths of a hatred that would last him the rest of his life.

"Go on, you lazy bastard, ask your computer!" the fat man, who seemed to have forgotten his Italian, spurred me on.

"You know what I have," I said to the chief. "I lead."

"Got a three in there?" asked Maldonado.

"And more," answered the chief.

"Then I want to redouble, gentlemen," said Maldonado, who was adding up the points and trying to stay calm.

"Let's play it out!" crowed Coluccini, putting everything he had on the line. He'd dealt the cards so perfectly that with Maldonado's redouble the entire bank would go to the Triunvirato team.

"Now they're trying to throw a scare into us," said the chief. "Don't chicken out, they're lying."

"I want to play out the hand," I said, to end the matter once and for all. The fat man tossed out a three, which I demolished with my ace of clubs. Then I played a spade and waited to see what would happen. The chief put down the seven of diamonds, and Coluccini, before playing, handed the speechmaker some papers, among which I recognized the multicolored check. "Give me an autograph," said the fat man, "as a souvenir."

As if he were joking, the man signed a blank sheet and also the yellow edge of the check. Coluccini put away the papers with a gesture of indifference and placed the ace of spades on the table. Then he raised his eyes toward the ship captain and graced him with a smile as wide as a slice of watermelon.

"Show them your card, Admiral."

It was the seven of spades, just as I had imagined, and the game was over because Coluccini really did pull out thirty-three. Maldonado turned the same shade of green as the cloth on the table and looked at me in a stupor. The chief's cigarette had gone out between his lips, and he was studying Maldonado as if he were looking over a prisoner before questioning him. Suddenly the fat man stood up, shook hands with everyone, and smiled at me in a friendly way.

"It's been a pleasure, *dottore*. Luck changes partners all the time so we can all be happy, isn't that so?"

"If you don't mind, I'll step into the men's room," I said.

"Naturally. Now you can turn off your computer," answered Coluccini.

"And the ace of spades?" Maldonado asked me, still standing there with his mouth hanging open. "What happened to the ace?"

"Wrap it up and send it on to Castelnuovo," I said as I went to the kitchen. Just as I had feared, the window was locked and I went to see how things stood with the skylight in the bathroom.

41 The bathroom was occupied, and out in the hall several men were waiting their turn. Seeing me walk up, a short, pimply man asked me if the meeting was over. I thought it best to say it wasn't, that both sides had made equally forceful arguments and that the end would be hard fought. All of them listened carefully, and a redhead who seemed nice told me to go first, that they could wait. Since the man inside was taking a long time, the redhead banged on the door and shouted for him to hurry, that the game was being held up because of him.

He came out almost immediately, buttoning his fly, and bowing to me as if he'd just crossed paths with the owner of Citibank. I thanked them all and locked the door behind me. The skylight was made of opaque glass and the ceiling was very high. I took off my shoes, tied them to my belt, and carefully climbed up on the toilet. From there I could reach the latch, but I realized it was going to be difficult to open the window.

There I was, pulling on the latch and trying not to slip, when I heard a murmur coming from the other side of the door. Then there was an uproar, and someone asked to speak with Engineer Rufino. I shouted that I'd be right out and hung on to the latch to scale the wall. Something unforeseen had happened, and I had to get out right away. I was just getting even with the skylight when I got a cramp that twisted my shoulder. The men in the hall began to batter the door, and the voice that before had called me engineer began to insult me from head to toe. I had reached the skylight when I heard Maldonado himself calling me a "motherless son of a bitch," "Buenos Aires bastard," and other names in the same style. The cramp slowed me down, but the door was about to give way, so it was not the time to invent clever quips. I kicked the glass and listened to the noise of the pieces falling to the ground; just when the redhead and the others knocked down the door, I gave a heave and threw myself out the window.

I landed on some garbage cans and knocked over a pile of empty bottles while the hens next-door raised hell. I was sweating more from the cramp than from fear, but luckily the pain subsided during my last tumble. When I stood up, all I felt was the urgent need to get out of there. I thought the chief would have called the patrol car and told myself the best thing to do was to climb up to the roofs next-door and look for a way to the other end of the block. I climbed up the wall in back and crawled to a shed made of sheet metal. The rooster was crowing his brains out, and I thought everyone would come out to see what was going on. While I caught my breath, I tried to imagine what could have happened to make the plan fall apart so quickly. I supposed that by then Coluccini was on his way to jail, and that this time there was nothing I could do for him.

I jumped onto a porch roof and from there climbed onto the roof of the house, which led to all the others on the street. I looked over at the street and saw a policeman running to the Rotary Club; that made me wonder if they hadn't had time to change the tire on the patrol car. I went from house to house until I could make out the lights on the chapel. At the corner, I looked down into a corral, where there were cars and horses no one was watching, and climbed down carefully, hugging the wall, pushing out with my feet so I wouldn't ruin the suit I'd come to like so much. When I reached the ground, I made sure there were no dogs running loose, and put on my shoes.

The horses shuffled around nervously but made no noise. No one had turned on a light, and the town seemed as dead as Junta Grande. I opened the wooden gate and, not knowing why, I untied the horses and drove them out into the street. Suddenly my fear vanished: I was once again in my childhood, and in my town, and everything I'd learned as an adult became useless. I

climbed onto an oil drum and from there jumped onto the back
of a worn-out pinto who'd stayed behind in the lot. The horse
let me do what I wanted so I took him out at a trot toward the
station.

I'd gone three or four blocks when I came upon a country man
riding a gray. He wore a wide-brimmed hat and had a ribbon
hung around his neck. He stopped to ask me for a light. We
looked at each other in silence under the street light, our horses
almost touching each other, and I handed him my lighter. He
was wearing black gaucho pants and had a flower in his button-
hole. He lit a half-smoked black tobacco cigarette and then
looked at me with some curiosity.

"Sorry to hold you up, sir, but I'm a little confused."

"Where you going?"

"To the mountains."

The streets were deserted, and I thought that perhaps we were
the last horsemen in this cheap little apocalypse.

"I can't help you."

"Thanks just the same."

"Forget you ever saw me, okay?"

"Sure."

He said good-bye touching the brim of his hat, and went
off with his spurs shining in the darkness. He had a number on
his back, as if he were returning from some rodeo. I went along
a dirt road until I came to the hedges where the Gordini was
hidden. In the distance, I saw people coming back from eating
at the chapel, and I left the horse so as not to attract attention.
The pinto stood at the side of the road as if he were lost, until I
gave him a little slap, and then he began to trot back to the
corral.

The car started right up, but I wondered if after all that had
happened I should follow Coluccini's instructions to the letter.
I decided to drive downtown, and when I reached the street
where the police station stood, I turned with the car in second
gear, ready to take off. The police car was still in the lot, but

they'd taken off the flat. At the door, the chief was talking with three patrolmen, all he had, probably. One of them saw the car passing and told the others as he turned on his flashlight. I paid no attention and went on with the lights out. I left the plaza behind and turned onto the avenue. I'd just decided to go back to the highway, abandon the car, and hide in the fields, when I saw Coluccini crossing the street, waving his arms. I turned on the light to be sure I wasn't mistaken: the fat man had lost his jacket and under his shirt all the bruises he'd accumulated during the trip were clearly visible.

42 He opened the door and, even before jumping into the seat, told me to take off, that they were right on his heels. I turned off the headlights and floored it. I almost sideswiped the statue of General Roca, but I managed to straighten out and keep going up the avenue. Meanwhile, Coluccini told me everything. Once we were on the highway, I turned on the headlights. We soon passed the watermelon truck: the driver waved as if he didn't know us, but this time we went right on by. He was sitting on a box, covered with rags, surrounded by a cloud of flies.

"Zárate, you can't imagine what I've been through," Coluccini wailed, almost in tears. "Those sons of bitches set the dogs on me."

"What happened?"

"The jacket your partner gave me had all the pockets ripped out, so as we all walked out to the ballroom, cards began falling out of my pockets. I'd take a step, and the ace of spades would fall to the floor, another step and a woman would kindly return my seven of hearts. . . . They almost killed me."

"You hadn't taken that into account?"

"No, what would ever make me think your partner had torn pockets?"

"There were two decks?"

"Of course, how do you think I managed to pull that thirty-three?"

"You're lucky you got away."

"I ran for it. Behind the coatroom, there was a hall that led to the tennis court. That's where they set the dogs on me. A pack, I swear."

"Got the check?"

"Of course."

"I let the air out of one of the tires on the police car."

"Really?" He looked at me in shock, as if he were discovering unsuspected virtues in me. "Zárate, you're a star!"

"Don't get too excited; when I passed by, they were fixing it."

"Shit, we've got to hide the car and lie low for a while!"

"Where can we put it? Around here you can see a rabbit five miles away."

"Go on, get off the road before the cops catch us. Where were you supposed to meet up with your partner?"

"Anywhere."

I slowed down and went along the shoulder slowly until I found a place where I could get down into the ditch. A few yards later, there was storm sewer that went under a bridge.

"Behind the wheel you're dangerous, Zárate. Let me take over."

"Whatever you say, but let's not cross the wire."

"I've heard that before someplace."

"Lem told you that. What else did he tell you?"

"He gave me the valise. He didn't seem like much of a talker."

"That story about how he fleeced the guys from Triunvirato wasn't true, was it?"

"To be frank with you, no. But I had to tell you something to get you going."

"Why did you lie to me? We aren't little kids."

"I had everything figured out. How could I have taken the torn pocket into account? Know how they looked at me?"

"I can imagine. Where's Lem's valise?"

"In the trunk. Come on, bring the key."

I didn't expect it to be there, but it was, along with another containing Coluccini's cassettes. Inside the valise there was more unused clothing, cans of sardines, and a few beers, the kind Lem left for me when we parted company at the Automobile Club. We took one valise each and packed the few useful things inside the car into them.

I was sure they weren't going to follow us because we hadn't taken anything and hadn't even managed to humiliate them. They could cancel the check with a simple phone call to Miami, but Coluccini still didn't know. I told him, with no reproaches, when he was down on all fours trying to see if his body could pass through the storm sewer. He seemed to take it calmly, but then I heard him let out a howl that echoed in the tunnel like the bellow of a wounded cow. After a while, he poked his head out, searched the darkness until he was looking me in the eye, and finally collapsed on one side, just like an animal in the slaughterhouse. He didn't move for a long time, and I had the impression he was searching for some memory among the few he had left or perhaps he was thinking about something that had nothing to do with us.

Lem's trousers were coming apart, and the fat man's milky buttocks and tanned back were peeking out through the split seam. I sat down on the valise and lit a cigarette. It was a matter of total indifference to me whether we stayed there or moved on. If I walked up to the highway, I'd be able to see the lights in Colonia Vela and imagine Alicia's night as she thought about Lem. We were all trapped in this spider web, walking along the edges like insects trying to make a desperate leap. In the silence, while I watched Coluccini stretched out on the ground, I reached the conclusion that something had to happen, something that would change everything.

I took off the ring I'd put on when I was with Alicia and threw it far away into a pond. The locusts were silently taking possession of the land, like invaders coming for the remains of a banquet which had come to an end. I caught one in the air and felt its wings and feet struggling against my fingers. One had almost cost me an eye back at the Automobile Club motel, so I took my revenge on this one, squeezing it in my fist until I hurt myself. I wiped my hand on the grass and felt strangely bad, as if what I'd done could change the luck of many people.

I don't remember how much time I spent sitting there looking at Coluccini. Finally I became convinced he must have been in the habit of collapsing, perhaps something he'd picked up from his profession; or maybe he was demoralized. In any case, I stopped thinking about him. I'd smoked several cigarettes when I heard a horse galloping along the shoulder. Suddenly the fat man emerged from his lethargy and dragged himself over to a thistle thicket, thinking he'd be safe there. I didn't move and waited for the rider to pass by, outlined in the darkness, heading for the mountains. I stepped up on the car's bumper and looked after him, but I couldn't see which number he had on his back. He stopped awhile opposite the gate, and then went trotting up the ditch.

Coluccini, who was still hysterical, asked in a whisper how many there were and if they were armed. I told him to calm down, that it was only a gaucho I'd met in Colonia Vela. Only then did he stand up, looking as devastated as an old chest of drawers. He said nothing; he shooed some locusts off his shirt, and checked through his torn pockets until he pulled out a handkerchief and the yellow check.

"Seriously now, you think they won't come?"

"What for? We aren't so important."

"If you knew the check wouldn't be of any use to us, why didn't you tell me earlier?"

"You wanted to do it, didn't you?"

He looked at the sky and then used the thistles to pull himself up to the highway.

"They've turned out the lights already."

"Want to drive for a while? At least we ate well."

"I'm sorry, Zárate. We almost screwed them, eh?" he shouted from up above, as if he were on stage.

I saw him cross the bridge, I heard him urinate, and then lost sight of him. The moon was decaying in its final quarter, half concealed by the clouds, and it was barely a warm breeze. I too walked away because I had to move my bowels. There, squatting in the weeds, I had the sensation that we no longer existed for anyone, not even for ourselves. We were satisfied with the promise of pulling a fast one or with a useless check. What attracted us was staring at our own toppled shadow—perhaps we would soon blend with it.

I wiped myself as best I could and went looking for rocks to brace the car wheels. I jammed them in hard against the rear wheels, and while I checked the battery I heard Coluccini's voice as he talked to me from the bridge. "Listen, was that stuff about the gaucho the truth?" he shouted.

"Of course. He said he was going to Chile."

"If he's going to bring the whole farm, I think he's going to have a tough time."

At first I didn't understand, but when I climbed up the embankment, I realized the gate was wide open and that the animals were escaping down the highway.

"Nice gaucho!" said Coluccini. "You can't trust anyone nowadays. . . . Let's get out of here, Zárate, before they put the blame on us."

43 He drove to the highway, dodged the cows that came through the gate and, as he accelerated, asked me to open him a beer. I turned on the light and opened two cans; the grasshoppers were jumping out onto the road, attracted by the headlights, and some splattered against the windshield. We closed the side windows and enjoyed the beer, not caring that it was warm. After a couple of hours, we came to a long curve that Coluccini followed with one finger on the wheel, and right after that, we crossed a bridge over a dry creek. Suddenly the road narrowed, and we saw that it abruptly ended in open country, with no signs anywhere.

Beyond an area of bare ground, we could see two dirt roads that spread apart like the two blades of a scissors. The fat man tossed his can out the window and slowed the car by downshifting, unable to decide which road to take. I saw him start to turn the wheel to one side and then to the other, but he ended up going straight ahead for a few more yards until he came to the creek. He tried to go around it and ended up in a swamp. The universal joint caught some branches that smacked against the chassis whenever he gave it the gas. Coluccini tried to get one wheel on solid ground, but the Gordini skidded to one side and got stuck in the bushes.

"Do you know how to tell where you are by the stars?" he asked, as if nothing had happened.

I got out of the car without looking at him and said I didn't. The headlights shone on the trunks of some eucalyptus trees; it looked like the end of the world, but just ahead, where the wires of the fence glinted, I caught sight of the discreet snout of Lem's Jaguar. I thought perhaps he'd had the same doubt we had at the end of the road and had stopped to sleep. I approached the car silently and saw he'd left the door open, but I didn't want to wake him up, so I walked away and leaned against a tree. Coluccini shouted to me, "There's your partner, ask him," and then he went off to stretch his legs at the side of the creek.

I was rather tired and no doubt would have fallen asleep if I hadn't noticed the shiny shoe hanging out of the Jaguar. It was only then it dawned on me that Lem hadn't awakened with all the noise. I jumped up and ran toward the car, but I could only make out the silhouette lying back in the seat. I spoke to him, but he didn't answer, and at that moment I understood what he meant when he called me at the Automobile Club.

I leaned over to turn on the ceiling light and found him, serious, his hair neatly combed, dressed in an impeccable suit and white shirt. He had a hole in his temple that made everything else seem superfluous. He'd had the good taste to open the doors so the bullet would exit without breaking anything. The photo of him as a boy, the one with him holding the top, was propped against the windshield, held there by the little cup I'd given him for luck.

Everything was in order on the dashboard, as if he'd made an inventory of the trip: the notebook with the red covers, the lipstick-stained cigarette butt, my roulette program, the receipt for a registered package sent to Barrante's family, and a recently opened pack of Camels. On the floor there was a glass and half a bottle of whiskey. I imagined him alone, with that forgettable, sad face, having his last drink, smoking a cigarette, looking for an answer out on the empty horizon. I looked more closely and could barely restrain my impulse to slap him; I was annoyed because I hadn't paid attention to his signals, because I didn't notice in time that the dice were loaded, that whatever his bet was it was always a loser. Maybe it was even before she said no at the crossing in Colonia Vela.

The dark suit was perfect for the occasion. He'd straightened the knot on his tie, but a sheet of notebook paper, folded in half, was sticking out of his pocket, where his handkerchief should have been. I walked around to the other side and sat next to him, as if I could still chat with him. I moved aside the hand holding the pistol and took out the paper to read it under the light. "I leave the car to you. Toss me anywhere. Yours affectionately, Lem." I put the paper away and put the handkerchief that went with the tie into the pocket. I supposed that to him it would have seemed the proper thing. At that moment, I remembered an old story by Bret Harte in which a man tries everything possible to save his partner from the gallows and then, after the sentence is carried out, loads him on a mule to bury him in the cemetery. I reread the message and told myself that if that was his last wish, I would toss him anywhere.

I took the weapon out of his hand and put it on the seat. Just then I realized I had to close his eyes. Suddenly I felt I'd been left all alone and looked up to get Coluccini's help. He was standing at the edge of the creek trying to guess which way the roads went, looking for a hole so he could jump off the spider web. I took the keys out of the Jaguar and called him as I walked to meet him. As soon as I got close, he realized Lem had given up the game. He took my hand, making an uncomfortable face, as if he were walking in on someone's wake, and expressed his sympathy.

"He killed himself," I said. "He shot himself."

He stared fixedly at me for an instant and then put his arm around me to take me for a walk. We went around the eucalyptus trees awhile, and he let me blow my nose a few times without consoling me or saying anything silly.

"Your partner was intelligent," he observed after a time. "He worked without a net and when he screwed up, he left without taking a bow.

"There comes a moment when you exit before the show becomes grotesque, Zárate. When you're in the spotlight, you realize it. The audience can be applauding its brains out, but when you're a real artist, you just know it's time."

44 Coluccini fell asleep on the Gordini's rear seat, and I stretched out under a tree to rest. At dawn, as the sky filled up with thick clouds, I heard the noise of a motor and then saw the Number 152 bus approaching the place where the road divided. The musicians got out, set up a tent, and made a fire. Finally I fell asleep, worn out with fatigue. The storm woke me up when the drops fell through the leaves and hit my face. I dreamed I was sleeping in the rain in another city with other people. I got up and took cover in the Jaguar, noticing at the same time that the gaucho, a poncho over his shoulder, was using a nearby eucalyptus as shelter.

His horse waited for him in the downpour, indifferent to everything, while the man tried to light a fire to brew some maté. When he saw me, he greeted me by touching his hat and then blew until a timid little flame, like that of a lighter, appeared among the dry branches. Lem's foot was still hanging out of the car, and so much water had gotten into his shoe that I went over and took it off, leaving it next to the other on the floor of the car. I sat next to him to smoke a cigarette and turned on the windshield wipers to watch the rain.

I imagined Coluccini must have been having nightmares and having a rough time because every so often the Gordini would rock as if someone were jumping on the bumper. I opened the glove compartment to see if I could find any other traces of Lem; there was nothing but the title to the car and a few loose aspirin. Maybe Lem had come looking for the kid in the photo, but like me he didn't know how to put up with himself. I wondered if the gaucho felt the same way, and it seemed to me he did, except that he'd just begun the trip. Through the window I saw him put out the fire and pack up the maté things. After that, he shook out the poncho that covered the number on his back and trotted past me. The rain flattened his hat; to cut the wire he had to get down and filthy his boots in the mud.

I drank a couple of whiskeys and went through Lem's pockets. One was torn and in the other I found money from every conceivable country, money he hadn't counted for the inventory. I kept the cup and the things he'd left on the dashboard and told myself that it was time to carry out his last wish. By pulling on his jacket, I got him into the passenger's seat; then I got behind the wheel, and, without saying anything to Coluccini, I drove back along the road to the bridge. I stopped near the rail, took off his watch, and pulled him out of the car, trying to keep him from banging into anything.

He was heavier than I thought, and I couldn't keep him from falling onto the pavement. I grabbed him by one arm and dragged him to throw him into the creek, but I slipped and we both fell down. I remembered Coluccini and how he was always on the ground and I began to laugh like a fool. I calculated that I wasn't going to be able to get him over the rail, so I lifted him up under the arms and sat him back in the Jaguar. He had an indifferent air to him but he was getting stiff and yellow. I turned the wheel, slipped it into drive, and pushed Lem's foot onto the accelerator. I got out of the way while the wheels spun, and finally the car went down into the creek, which now had water in it. Lem's world, or at least as much of it as he'd wanted to show me, disappeared from sight.

As the sun came up, I started walking along the creek, a shortcut to where Coluccini was. The current carried sunflowers and tree branches; I walked a good distance and then came upon a dead cow that blocked my path.

I went down the bank and waded, the water up to my knees. For a moment I thought I was hearing thunder, then I went around a curve and saw a jeep crossing along the edge of the creek. A man perched on top of the spare tire carried a whip and directed things by shouting. Before reaching the bridge, he turned around and paused to calculate what kind of enemy he had before him. He stood up for a minute, and the driver jumped out shouting something I didn't understand. I waded to the shore to see him better, and even though he had no uniform left, it was clear he was a soldier.

The jeep was a pile of rusty scrap-iron that shook like a leaf and gave off black smoke. The man pointed toward where I'd crashed the Jaguar and went back to his place at the wheel. The jeep instantly went down the embankment, and I heard the noise of crumpling sheet metal and smashing glass. When it came back, I realized they were going to take it out on me, so I decided to stand still with my hands up.

Judging by its looks, the jeep was World War II vintage, and it hadn't been painted since then. For identification purposes, they'd tied a blue and white National Petroleum Corporation oil can to the barrel of their machine gun. The officer had gray hair like Lem's, but he was older and looked like a jerk. He flexed his knees and stood up to look at me carefully through his binoculars. After a while he shouted to me to put my hands down and stand at ease. I obeyed and asked him if he'd let me light a cigarette, but he pretended not to listen. So I took out the pack, and that enraged him; he waded to shore and, soaking wet, strode up to within an inch of my nose, the way they did in boot camp.

"Sing the national anthem!" he shouted. "And I want to hear it!"

I bellowed it out, and when he'd heard it all, he took two steps back and saluted me respectfully. It was impossible to make out his rank, and his uniform was a combination of gaucho trousers and a faded jacket. On his chest he wore some decorations, all made by hand from pieces of wood and old cans.

"This is a military zone, damn it! Can't you read?"

"There are no signs," I answered, without lowering my voice.

"They were stolen," he admitted with a gesture of disgust. "What classification were you assigned, soldier?"

"The highest, seventh, I think. Is it possible?"

He liked being put to the test. He tapped his whip against his boots, stepped back a few more steps, and measured me with his eyes.

"Correct," he said, turning around to shout an order: "Turn off the motor, man!"

The noise abated, and a fortyish-looking man got out of the jeep: he wore a handkerchief on his head and looked as if he'd never seen a civilian.

"I remind you that this is the Hour of the Fatherland, General!" he shouted, standing there awaiting orders. The other man looked up at the rainy sky, squinted at his pocketwatch, and pointed to something lost in the mist.

"Fall in," he told me. "We have to raise the flag."

"Is the regiment far away?"

"Regiment! We're as naked as General San Martín when he crossed the Andes, can't you see? Did you ever serve in a color guard?"

"No, but I remember how it was done. So I guess I did."

"Come with me, then. Do you know what day this is?"

"No, General. I've lost count."

"It's the twenty-fifth of May, Independence Day."

"May's during the fall, isn't it?"

"It's when our hearts swell, soldier."

"They'd give us chocolate, I remember."

"That much I don't have. We've got boiled maté and crackers."

He saluted again and invited me to get into the jeep. I thought Coluccini wouldn't be upset if I took my time and got in. The rain had stopped, but there was a mist that made everything confused. The driver made his way over the flattest ground, where there was almost no grass, following the creek. The general shouted something I couldn't hear because of the noise, and I lit a cigarette without asking permission.

Eventually we reached a hollow which they'd set up as if it were a command post. At the bottom there was a kind of Indian encampment made of steer hides, and in the widest part they'd made a space to park the jeep. On the other side, I saw some wooden crosses stuck into the ground and a post they used as a flagpole. Beyond began a field of sunflowers. The jeep stopped near the cemetery, and the general helped me get out, as if he were younger than I.

"Has it been a long time since anyone's come by?" I asked.

"That's what I've been asking you about, soldier. If you saw anything of the infantry."

"I haven't seen a thing. Did they abandon you?"

"They must have been disbanded, I don't know. One day we woke up and they weren't there."

"Did that happen a long time ago?"

"Quite a long time ago. I was still a captain, so you can just imagine."

"How many of you are left?"

"Just the two of us. The old officer corps passed on."

"Excuse me, General, are you sure today is May twenty-fifth?"

"Got something against it?"

"No, nothing."

"All right then, let's get on with the ceremony."

I saluted him and took charge of the flag the driver handed me. He must have been a major or a lieutenant colonel; it was impossible to tell because the rain had washed away his inked-in rank. He too was wearing a decoration made of rusty tin and a crucifix. All that remained of the flag was the traces of the blue bands, but the sun had disappeared. I went to the post and came to attention, trying to make my heels click properly. Behind me, the driver tooted the bugle, and then there was a silence like a lost battle. The sky suddenly darkened, and while I pulled on the cord and the flag went up, the first waves of locusts arrived.

46 By the time the flag reached the top of the pole, the sky was black. I did an about-face and saluted, ready to begin the national anthem, but the general looked nervous, distracted from the national holiday. The cloud of locusts began to descend onto the fields, and when everything was dark, the general ordered a retreat. The other officer dove for the embankment; I didn't know which way to go, but the general never lost his composure and ordered me to follow him. We had to cover our eyes because the insects were flying every which way, slamming into every part of our bodies. The general walked down into the entrenchment swinging his whip, slapping his legs, enveloped in a swarm of wasps fleeing in the same direction.

As we ran, we saw the other officer set fire to one of the tents as he pointed to the fields devastated by the plague. The general took me by the arm and pushed me toward a tent that must have been his command post. Inside, there were a few lost locusts, but we immediately batted them down, and the driver closed off the entryway with a burlap sack. Now we were in darkness, and the noise coming from outside was like the furious spatter of rain. It seemed the general was clearing his throat to spit something out, so I again asked permission to smoke.

"Shit, what a day, Lieutenant!" he answered, spitting in no particular direction.

"The man's too old for that, General," said the other. "Make him a captain; after all, he earned it."

"Don't you think you're giving a lot of orders, Major? Why did you set that fire without being ordered to do so?"

"That was the appropriate action, sir. Article Forty-seven: 'Against plague, fire.' "

"You aren't going to want a medal for having a good memory too, are you?"

"No, General. If you promote him to captain, we'll have the ceremony tomorrow."

"Stay and we'll celebrate, Lieutenant."

"No, I'm just passing through."

"All right, but you'll have to explain what your mission is. Do you know what the hell is going on in the outside world?"

"I think it's falling apart, General."

"That remains to be seen. I haven't given up yet."

"Were you ever in a war?"

"No. I was left in command of a battalion and had to take care of things on my own. Let's see, Major—do the regulations allow us to assign this man a mission?"

"Yes, General. Article Eighty-three, subparagraph nine: 'Grave or desperate situation.' If he's a lieutenant, it applies."

"We had a lieutenant around here, a guy named Heredia, who came from some war or other. You always had it in for him, Major."

"That snotnose kid. I told you he was going to rob the tank."

"The radio, the boots, he took everything."

"Suppose someday you find the infantry, General?" I asked.

"That's just what your mission is. Do you know what General Belgrano did at Ayohuma?"

"He rallied the troops and retreated," I answered.

"Very good. Before I withdraw, I have to regroup the battalion."

"I don't remember who revolted over in Olavarría."

"Quintana, General," said the other man. "It was in Azul."

"General Quintana. He kicked up a hell of a row, and they ordered us over there. I was a captain."

"No," interrupted the other. "You were a major, and I was a lieutenant."

"Anyway, we had a firefight. Colonel Vianini gave up, but we kept going. I don't know why. Later, lots of senior officers died, and we had to keep rising in rank."

"We kept going because that ass Fulco wanted to try out the flares," said the major.

"By now he must be on the General Staff. He was a good officer. Go on, Major, brew up some maté."

"It's the last bag, I'm warning you."

"The last one! It's been the last one for twenty years!"

"Know what I was just remembering, General?" asked the major. "When my aunt would send me cookies at school."

"What would she say now, eh? Like my wife, God knows what she's thinking."

"They might even be looking for you both," I said, pushing aside the burlap sack to see if the locusts were still there. There was no more noise, but because we were talking in the darkness, it felt as if all the voices were coming out of me.

"A helicopter flew over quite a while back, but they must have confused us with someone else, and that's when we lost the little cannon."

"What a shot the man was," said the major. "He put a round right on the detonator. Nothing was left."

"He was using a seventy-millimeter gun. I'll never forget the look on Meinak's face. You might think I gave up right then and there, but they never came back."

"Who is Meinak?"

"He was our artillery officer. He's buried with the others.

Do you know what San Martín did at the battle of Cancha Rayada?"

"With all due respect, General, you only remember defeats," I pointed out.

"It's that defeats are more heroic. Everyone's going to remember our campaign; it'll be taught in schools."

"Who is the enemy now?"

"Anyone who leaves the road."

"There are no more locusts."

"Well, we've gone through worse things. Drink a few matés, because we're going to begin maneuvers."

"With your permission, I'll just be on my way, General?"

"Way? What way, Lieutenant? Or do you think we're here on vacation?"

"I'll go along the creek. What is my mission?"

"If you find the infantry, get right back here."

"My aunt is in Santa Fé," said the other man, moving around in the darkness. "Tell her to stop sending cookies. God knows who's receiving them instead of me."

"Forget it, Major," said the general, "don't deprive her of her illusion."

"In that case, don't. Don't tell her anything."

I flicked on my lighter and pushed aside the burlap sack to go out. They came after me, and we found the fields picked clean. It was like a perfectly pressed sheet stretched out all the way to the horizon.

"Bye-bye harvest," said the major, picking up his bugle, which shone as if he'd just shined it. The general held out a big, ruined hand and then saluted me.

"Carry out your orders, Lieutenant. And if you don't, may the Fatherland settle accounts with you or something like that. I don't remember what number that was in the military code."

"Rest assured, General," I said. "They'll come."

As I made my way along the bank of the stream, I heard the

bugle bidding me farewell, and I turned around to wave to them. The locusts had passed, and there was nothing left on their flagpole.

47 Along the way, I found the remains of three smashed-up cars and a truck. The junk had been tossed into the streambed; I wasn't in the mood to see what there was between the layers of metal. They'd been thrown there a long time ago, and nothing of what was left had any value. Around me I saw only bare earth under a gray sky. My wet clothes were cumbersome, so even though I'd sneezed a few times I took off my jacket and tie. According to Lem's watch, it was 10:20 on a Tuesday, but I had no certainty that either the day or the time was correct. The stream made a few eccentric twists and turns on the ever-flat ground; now that the locusts had passed through, I could no longer use the tree tops as a guide. I walked for a couple of hours until I came to an abandoned shed made of sheet metal and some railway tracks that stopped there.

I got undressed and went to sleep next to the entrance, protected from the wind, which was beginning to pick up. When I awakened, I saw a reddish cat studying me from a water tank. At another time, the tank had been used to supply steam engines with water, but now it was split open from top to bottom. For an instant I wondered if I was lost, but I was sure that if I followed the stream, I'd reach the place where Coluccini was parked. Unless that was another stream. In any case, I couldn't go back. I realized that I'd slept a long time because this was a new day, more bright and sunny. I went over to wash in a drum where rainwater had collected. The ground was covered with dead lizards, and lost horseflies buzzed in the air. As I got dressed to go looking for the fat man, I felt I was in the same situation as in the first days, lost and hungry.

The road had forked there too; I could go on following the stream or take the road that went on straight as far as I could see. I chose the stream and went along its bank at a good pace, without becoming distracted, thinking that with a little luck I might be able to catch an armadillo to cook that night. I found nothing. All the plants were dried out, and there were no animals except the cat, who was following me as if I knew the way. At sundown, I spotted the Gordini's hood and ran toward it. The musicians were no longer there, and I didn't find Coluccini either. The car's wheels were sunk in the clay, and from the tracks, I could see that the fat man had tried in vain to free it.

He'd left the lights on, so the battery was dead. He'd taken the valise containing the videos, which must have been his only treasure. On the dashboard there were a few splattered locusts. The food was rotten, but there was a little cheese that had survived the heat and a few cans of beer tossed onto the floor. I made myself comfortable behind the steering wheel and contemplated the sunset. I imagined the general and the major must have been watching it too. I felt around in the glove compartment and found the dark glasses, a pack of cards, and some pieces of paper filthy with grease. They were newspaper articles and old circus programs Coluccini hadn't shown me. I put them away and went to open the trunk to see if he'd taken Lem's things as well. Everything was in its place: clothes, cigarettes, the things necessary for a trip. I took advantage of the last rays of sunlight to shave with some good cream and change clothes. Perhaps Coluccini thought I'd abandoned him and had gone on alone carrying the videos.

I took my bag and walked toward the crossroads. The two roads looked identical, and I decided to take whichever one came up according to the little cup. I tossed it up in the air behind my back, and when it landed, I followed it with my eyes until it stopped a few yards beyond. I went that way, which took me into the sunset, and told myself that sooner or later someone would pass by whom I could ask to drop me off at the next traffic circle. I was well-dressed and looked like a respectable person who'd had car trouble. So I walked along as it got darker and darker, so much so that I could barely make out the bushes invading the road. It was midnight when I came to a railway crossing, where I sat down to rest. I asked myself if the gaucho from Colonia Vela would have bothered to mail the letter to my daughter and told myself he would, that someday at another mailbox I'd find her answer.

As I looked at the stars, I saw a light moving in the distance, a long way down the line. For a while, it stopped in one place, and then it began to come closer, not making a sound. I lit a cigarette and leaned back to wait. After a bit, I saw Coluccini's silhouette carrying a valise. He came toward me smiling. When he saw me, he raised a squarish lantern, the kind railroad signalmen use, and stood still as if he were waiting for me to give him a welcome. He was covered with mud, and I assumed he had fallen into a puddle. I told him to sit down and offered him a beer, but he said he wasn't thirsty. He made himself comfortable on top of the valise and stretched his feet without taking off his torn shoes.

"You're not going to believe me," he said, "but I just saw Jesus Christ in person."

"I believe you."

"He was on the cross and shouted out, *'Coluccini! Coluccini!'* Just imagine, I've seen everything, but I was scared out of my wits."

"Are you a believer?"

"No, and that was the first thing I told him. It was raining like hell, and all of a sudden I don't know what happened but I can tell you for sure everything began to shake."

"Locusts," I told him. "A plague passed over."

"It could be. You'd gone to take care of your partner, and suddenly in the lightning flashes I see the cross and Christ, who starts calling me. At the beginning I thought I knew him from one of my road tours, because there are lots of guys who turn a buck that way, but no, I'd never seen this one before. '*Coluccini!*' he shouted to me, '*Coluccini!*' So I went over to him and asked, 'Coluccini what?' 'Coluccini Antonio,' he says from up there. I didn't know what to do, if I should go down on my knees or run away. 'What are you doing around here?' he asks. 'You're always turning up where you don't belong.' "

"You must have been hallucinating."

"What do I know, an incredible storm was going on. 'Old sinner,' he said to me, 'may God bless you!' "

"And then?"

"Nothing. '*L'avventura è finita!*' he shouted. And then he started to shake all over. I think I fainted, and I really mean that."

"Still going to Bolivia?"

"More than ever now. What about you?"

"I don't know. Every time I meet someone, they give me a job to do. Now I have to look for some lost infantry."

"Stay here, then. Go looking for oil. Right around here there's a train."

"I double you, Coluccini."

He looked at me with a beatific smile. The lantern shone on us from the railroad ties and made the rails glisten on the bare earth.

"I can't lose anymore, Zárate. I'll be in Bolivia, and my memories will be mine again. So I redouble you."

"Will you bet your Jesus Christ?"

"If you put up your infantry."

"Where'd you get that lantern?"

"From the train." He pointed behind him. "I think they're waiting for you."

"All right," I said, "deal," taking out the cards.

48 I ended up dealing, but he won just the same, pulling a thirty-three. He was still smiling and looked so confident that for the first time I thought he really would get to Bolivia. Maybe he'd found the hole in the spider web and was inviting me to jump, even though we'd be going in different directions. I'd done my duty with Lem, and now Coluccini was taking away my memory of the general and his lost infantry.

I was even with everyone; maybe someday I'd be even with myself. I put away the cards and offered him the little cup so he'd remember me when he was off in the jungle. He refused, telling me to keep it because I was going to need it, and he raised the lantern to look down the road that awaited him. On both sides, the wire fence had fallen down, and now it was possible to walk over the fields as if they were a desert. He told me he was sorry to abandon the Gordini, but the motor had burned out when he tried to get it out of the swamp.

"I told you it was time to change the oil."

"Yes, you always remembered things like that. If you get to Bolivia some day, ask for me. Everyone's going to know me."

"Don't get into trouble, Coluccini. Who knows if the guy on the cross wasn't a con man. I think he shouted something else in the Bible."

"What does that matter, Zárate? He shouts whatever it is you need."

"My name isn't Zárate."

"You never did tell me what your name is. Why don't you write to your daughter and tell her the truth? Get up the courage and do it."

"If I find a mailbox . . . I can tell her I had a friend who could fly and who always drew the cards he wanted."

"Don't tell her things went badly for me. Tell her people applauded me."

"But you asked me to tell her the truth."

"We went a good way together, Zárate, and you don't know anything about me. Just put in some applause for me, because I've got a long road in front of me."

"You know which way to go?"

"When you settle your account with all this, you're going to know too. Get on the train and write that letter. Don't weaken and don't put your foot on the brake. And if you should ever decide to give up the game, make sure there's someone to toss you away too. It's not a good idea to stay around getting in the way."

"Is there really a train?"

"Over that way." He pointed to a place in the darkness. "Want me to make you a map so you'll get there?"

"No, it's about time I started finding my own way."

"If you find it, toot the whistle. Is the cat going with you?"

I turned around and saw the reddish cat looking at us, peeking out from behind the tracks.

"I don't know, he's been following me since last night. It's been a pleasure to know you, Coluccini."

"The pleasure is all mine." He got up to shake hands with me. "That suit looks good on you."

I was going to give him the newspaper clippings I'd found in the car, but I thought that if he'd left them it was because he didn't need them. I insisted he keep the little cup, which he finally accepted, putting it in a possibly ripped pocket. He told me to take the lantern, and we hugged each other. I left him there with his smile still on him, and that made me feel better. He looked like a beggar, and it wasn't going to be easy for him to get someone to pick him up. I told myself that, who knows, the two of us might just be getting somewhere. I walked over the ties, calculating the distance so I wouldn't trip because the embankment was getting steeper and steeper. The lantern gave off a very tenuous, yellow light, barely adequate for me to sense the company of the cat, who was in front of me. I walked all night, and when it finally began to get light, I could make out the shape of a very long train on a siding. The departure sign was in the GO position and the light was green, but I didn't see anyone in the locomotive and the cars' curtains were drawn. I put out the lantern and went to see if the engineer was asleep. Before I got on, I clapped my hands, but there was no answer, and in the cabin of the engine I found only a few dead locusts and a rail map stuck onto the controls. It was due to pull out at eight, but it didn't say which day, and I didn't know what the date was. I pulled a cord to toot the whistle, as the fat man had asked me, and waited to see if anyone came. All that could be heard was the air whistling through the broken windows. I slid down the embankment and ran to the caboose, but it too was empty. The cat jumped up the embankment and stood there looking at the dry bushes being carried along by the wind. I pushed aside the weeds that had tangled around my legs, carried my bag to the last car, and opened all the windows so the sun would come in. Then I took out the last beer and sat down to wait for the train to pull out.

A Note About the Author

Osvaldo Soriano was born in 1943 in Mar del Plata, Argentina. He lived and worked in Buenos Aires until 1976, when the military took over the government. For the next eight years he lived in exile in Brussels and then Paris. In 1984, after a civilian democracy was restored to power, Soriano returned to live in Buenos Aires. He has written six novels, of which *A Funny Dirty Little War*, *Winter Quarters*, and *Shadows* have been translated into English.

A Note on the Type

The text of this book is set in Garamond No. 3. It is not a true copy of any of the designs of Claude Garamond (1480–1561), but an adaptation of his types, which set the European standard for two centuries. It probably owes as much to the designs of Jean Jannon, a Protestant printer working in Sedan in the early seventeenth century, who had worked with Garamond's romans earlier, in Paris, and who was denied their use because of the Catholic censorship. Jannon's matrices came into the possession of the Imprimerie Nationale, where they were thought to be by Garamond himself, and so described when the Imprimerie revived the type in 1900. This particular version is based on an adaptation by Morris Fuller Benton.

Composed by
Crane Typesetting Service,
West Barnstable, Massachusetts
Printed and bound by
Arcata Graphics/Martinsburg,
Martinsburg, West Virginia
Designed by Anthea Lingeman